TRISTAN

TRISTAN

ROGUE ANGELS
BOOK THREE

LILITH DARVILLE

eBook ISBN: 978-1-998127-25-2
Paperback ISBN: 978-1-998127-26-9

Cover Design by Atra Luna Design (www.atraluna.de)
Editing by Maggie Morris, The Indie Editor (www.indieeditor.ca)
Formatting by Kate Tilton's Author Services, LLC (www.katetilton.com)

BLACK ROSE AND THE THREE PRINCES

THE FAIRY TALE CONTINUES . . .

The connection was instant the moment they met. Atroyel, using a rock musician's body as his vessel, became her guardian angel, protecting and shielding her from abuse to the best of his limited ability while she grew into a young woman and gave him her love. But, like the princes, Syrael searched ceaselessly for the face in the mirror. Each time his mirror swept the Earth realm, Atroyel's powers shielded Black Rose. However, his essence weakened with every pass, and after a two-year struggle, his mortal vessel died, forcing Atroyel to ascend back to Bardo... leaving Black Rose exposed to the archangel's all-seeing magic mirror.

CASSIEL

"Fuck!" Shame and fear consume me as I bounce off the curtain of light surrounding my brothers and Aleah as a divine mating bond binds the three of them. I arrive a split second too late to stop Aleah from stealing my brothers from me. Now, it's up to me to save them. And myself. I refuse to take too close a look at precisely what I'm saving them from. If I do that, I might have to admit a truth or two I refuse to acknowledge.

Rage swamps over me as I watch the three of them linked, locked and awash in divine love. Love and desire bleed through our triplet link in nauseating quantities. This couldn't have happened; shouldn't have happened. Nothing was supposed to be strong enough to shatter the triplet bond between the royal princes of the Blue Vale.

Maybe Lord Syrael was right about her.

Where the fuck did that come from? I give my head a shake. Ever since Aleah rescued that child slave Tommy, I've been getting flashes better left forgotten.

Fueled by anger that's building to an inferno, I stalk from the room. One of us has to be fucking responsible here, and as usual, that job falls on my shoulders. Aleah's detailed agenda that she was so fucking kind to share with us advises she's touring some private membership club for her gods-damned article. It falls to me to do the fucking prework my brothers should have done. The fucking assholes should know better than let their libidos take priority over the mission to protect Aleah from Lord Syrael at all costs.

"Turn her over to me. You'll get your brothers back, and I'll set you free."

I could swear I hear a deep voice whispering those words in my head, but the thought is gone before I can grasp it. Yet it's happening more and more, these dark threads filtering through my thoughts. Then there's the constant hum of heat from our triplet link that's taken hold of my junk. It's jerking me one way and the dark threads another. It's enough to make an angel batshit crazy and lets me know I *need* to get laid. I can kill the proverbial two birds with one visit to Pandemonium—scout the location and scene with a hot sub.

I stop by my assigned bedroom to take off my jacket and shed my tie in a nod to a more casual look. Wearing one of my signature custom suits to scene at a sex club in the middle of the night is more than a bit of overkill. I'll be there to survey, not announce my presence, and the high-noon gunslinger look of the 1920's style clothing I favor makes a statement. So, I tone it down. Many there will be wearing fetish gear, but that's not my style.

Raphael waits near the door as I step into the main hall, my long outer coat slung carefully over his extended arm.

"Thank you." I stride forward, and he holds the coat open for me to shrug on. Seeing the caretaker waiting as if he reads my mind startles me, but I'm a master at hiding my reactions from everyone, friend or foe.

Raphael raises his palm, and a small vial appears. The nectar inside the vial cloaks our divine grace and magic.

I shake my head and wave a hand, dismissing the idea. "Thanks, but I won't be needing that." My tone makes it clear this is not up for discussion. I have more than enough power to suppress my magic, making it undetectable. If I choose to.

Raphael bows his head slightly and the vial disappears. "As you wish."

"I'll be at the Pandemonium club getting us registered. I'll be back in a couple of hours." I open a portal before he can argue with me and step through into the shadows outside of the private sex club. After explaining my visit to reception, a "serving wench" named Darcy escorts me around the premises. She points out various rooms and explains the pandemic protocols they practice, eventually stopping in the primary dungeon. The social area is full of people in various stages of undress and fetish gear chatting and watching the scenes in the adjoining play area. My attention is immediately drawn to the bondage equipment on a far wall as a large man sidles up beside me.

"Most of the furniture is unique and custom-built for The Woodshed." The man is shorter than me, but his commanding presence quickly identifies him as a Dom. "My name is Master Zazz. Welcome to our dungeon. The front desk tells me Cyrus Stone referred you to us." The inflection in his tone doesn't rise, but there's no doubt the man expects an answer. He gives Darcy a nod, and she strides off toward the reception area.

"Indirectly, yes." I match my tone to his. "I'm here to scout the location on behalf of Mosaic Magazine and their contributor, Aleah Hunter. She's writing a feature series on Cyrus Stone and his Pleasure Palace." I stop short of opining on how a man with so little imagination can run a sex empire.

Zazz, massive arms crossed over his barrel chest, stares and waits. I stifle my impatience. Getting on this guy's wrong side will no doubt piss Aleah right off. The thought of her petite body facing off with me once again without fear makes my cock go rock hard. I push the thought away needing to focus on the play before me.

"Are those modified St. Andrew's Crosses?" I point to the bondage furniture lining the wall. Since flogging and whipping are my favorite forms of impact play, I'm particularly interested in bondage furniture. And having Aleah's naked body splayed out on it. Again, my cock goes harder still, and I pull my long coat closed. Unlike the exhibitionists in the crowd, I prefer to choose how I display myself in public.

Zazz's lips quirk into a smile as if letting me know I'm not fooling him for a second. He's seen it all before and then some, I have no doubt. He nods. "The design is a hybrid between a St. Andrew's Cross and another piece we developed called the Stickman. They're comfortable for your bottom and very stable."

I give a nod to acknowledge his subtle identification of a fellow Dom. "I look forward to giving it a try."

The tour continues, and Zazz points out various points of evident pride. I listen impatiently as he holds forth about the shibari rigs and rope play, but that's Tristan's kink, not mine. However, the custom spanking benches do capture my attention. Another image of Aleah, this time kneeling on the red leather, legs spread wide on the spanking bench, keeps my cock standing at attention.

After noting the bootblack stand for later use, Zazz spends a few moments pointing out the features of an updated suspension cage. Again, not my usual kink as I have no patience for protracted punishment play.

Darcy comes up behind Zazz and stands demurely, head down in submission until he gestures for her to speak. She slides closer and whispers in his ear.

"Ah, good," Zazz says. "Sensei Master Stone happens to be

on the premises, and he's eager to meet one of the Mosaic Magazine's entourage."

My heart rate accelerates at the mention of his name. I put it down to Zazz's unusual use of the title *sensei master*. The title lets me know that Cyrus Stone considers himself a BDSM king.

Zazz leads the way down a long hall, opens the door to a private playroom and steps back, gesturing for me to go inside. Eager to meet the kingpin and set the ground rules, I walk forward, barely registering the door closing behind me.

A large man sits on an oversized padded chair upon a raised platform, like a throne on a dais. Muscular legs are spread wide, and a hairy forearm sits on each throne's arm, a bullwhip curled in one hand. As our eyes meet, his glow with an ethereal black light. Images of the time when he had guardianship over me and my brothers comes flooding back. It's as if he rips away the bandage hiding the festering boil of dark magic that he planted in my soul to make me submit to being a plaything for him and his friends. Fear and loathing swarm through me as his dark power pours over me, taking control of my muscles and mind.

"Kneel, Cassiel. Bow to your master." His deep voice brings back another torrent of images from the torture I endured as a child. Torture I suffered at the hands of him and his patrons to save my brothers from a similar fate. I lock my knees, refusing to bow, ignoring the fear choking off my air supply. I'm no longer that boy.

I hear the snap a split second before the pain hits the tender spot at the back of my knees. I drop to the floor, bowing to Cyrus Stone.

2

CASSIEL

Terror bolts through me as one of Lord Syrael's henchmen slams my forehead to the floor. Searing agony spiders through my head, competing with the pain in the back of my legs. Lord Syrael used his expert whip skills to strike where my hamstrings meet the backs of my knees, causing angry heat to run upward from there into my glutes. Hate joins the fear as the bastard chuckles.

"Well, well, well. It's been a hot decade, Cassiel, but it was only a matter of time. Welcome back to the fold. Now, let's get down to business." Lord Syrael's tone darkens. "Let's have a look at you."

Nausea follows the fear as my head snaps up and Lord Syrael's onyx eyes drill through me.

"I sent you boys to recover something that belongs to me. Where is it?" He coils the whip around his hand as if readying for another strike.

Another bolt of hatred tears through my system at the way he refers to Aleah. One of his belongings. One of his pets. *Just like me.* "If you're referring to Black Rose, she's with the Druids, sensei." I bite the words out, determined not to let this bastard get the best of me despite knowing I've already lost.

Lord Syrael gets off his throne and crosses the floor, stopping when he's about a foot in front of me. The guard yanks my head back, so I have no choice but to look at the sensei master. He studies me for a long moment as his black eyes laser through me. Finally, he frowns as if he's not happy with what he sees and snaps his fingers. On cue, a woman wearing nothing but a harness and collar steps forward and holds out a bowl, head bowed in total submission. After choosing what looks like a tiny slug, he dangles it in the air and says, "*àithne tha thu a 'dol a-mach agus purge." I command thee, go forth and purge.* Lord Syrael grabs my jaw and forces my mouth open.

"Before we begin, let's get rid of the taint of divine magic." He drops the slug into my mouth. "This parasite will reverse the effects of the light and return your memory tenfold."

My attempts to close my throat are futile, and the fucking thing slides down my esophagus. I start to gag, but the guard holds my head rigid while Lord Syrael clamps my mouth shut, making it impossible for me to do anything but swallow. Moments later, it's as if the slug replicates and spreads throughout my body, leaving needle-sharp pain and darkness trailing in its wake like storm clouds consuming the light. After several agonizing minutes, the pain subsides into a kind of deep despair. The hard shell around my heart makes it difficult to take a deep breath, so I settle with several shallow ones.

"First, little Cassiel, you'll receive your punishment. Sadly, I'll have to make it particularly painful to remind you of your place." Lord Syrael snaps the whip, and the sound takes me back to memories of when I was a plaything at his infamous sex parties. Bile rises in my throat, but I swallow it down. I need to stay strong, just like all those years ago. For my brothers. *For Aleah.* I slam the door shut on thoughts of them.

Lord Syrael can read minds, and I refuse to let his evil near even the thought of those I care for.

"This will serve as a little reminder of what lies ahead if you fail me," Lord Syrael says. A stunning fae wearing a large strap-on and holding a long whip steps out of the shadows and takes a position beside him. I gasp as light hits her face, and I recognize her. Flare Sugartree, the fae princess who stole and almost destroyed my heart, gives me a smile that doesn't reach her cold purple eyes. I start as I realize the white designs that used to be part of her irises are now the same onyx as Lord Syrael's. As she rakes her eyes over me, she licks her lips in anticipation, giving me a moment to wonder why she's here on Earth. Typically, the fae live in a dimension that keeps them separate from humanity, but Lord Syrael probably demanded her presence for the sole purpose of humiliating me.

"Now, let's get this scene started," Lord Syrael says as two of his men wheel a spanking bench into the center of the room and lock it in place. A slight nod of his chin and the bastard holding me jerks me to my feet.

"Don't fight my little pet, Cassiel. The slugs are programmed to attack any attempts to stop their clean-up of divine magic to madness. Fight them, and you'll end up mad as a hatter." Lord Syrael throws his hair back and booms out a laugh at his bad joke. It stops as sharply as it started, and he turns his attention back to me.

"My little parasite will help you to break Aleah's will. I want her ready to submit when you bring her to me," Lord Syrael says.

"And just how do you propose I do that?" I spit back.

"It shouldn't take you long to remember the mind games we used to play using self-doubt to penetrate defenses. The parasites will help with that. Now, would you like to undress, or would you rather have my men do it for you?" Lord

Syrael's mild tone doesn't deceive me. If I allow his men to do it, I'll have many more bruises than any whipping will give me. I assume Lord Syrael isn't about to disable me before I deliver his grand prize, but he's also been known to turn a blind eye while his men land a couple of solid punches to the kidneys or a knee to the tailbone. Nothing crippling but resulting in weeks of pain and misery. Biting back my anger, I remove my clothing, folding it neatly on the floor, delaying the inevitable for a few precious seconds longer.

When I look up, Lord Syrael gestures toward the bench. I glance toward the door where two of the lord's men stand guard.

"Don't worry. Zazz knows better than to disturb me while I'm in my private playroom." Cords of power stream from Lord Syrael's fingers lashing me to the bench spread-eagle, face first. There's no mention of a safe word as he takes his place before me. I resort to taking more shallow breaths trying to stop my heart from shattering into the stratosphere.

"Look at me."

The slugs make me incapable of fighting his power—my head snaps up at his command. *Crack!* The singletail whip explodes like lightning from his hand and snakes through the air like one of Medusa's hairs. A shudder slips free as I remember just how skilled Lord Syrael was in this kind of extreme impact play, how much he liked to use the whip to draw a pattern of razor cuts across my ass and thighs. The fucking demon lord smiles at my involuntary reaction. I wish for just one second that I could reach for that glimmer of divine light I'd seen while with Aleah. But if I do that, Lord Syrael will see it and take possession of the link. If only I could see my brothers one more time before the demon lord's evil turns me into a puppet who will betray them.

The guard drops my head, and Lord Syrael moves out of

my field of vision, and I almost feel him widen his stance and brace himself to deliver the second blow. I block out everything but the pain, determined to stop Syrael from stealing what remains of our triplet connection from me. *Crack! Crack!* The blows rain down on me, and soon what can only be blood droplets trickle down my thighs. I try to lean into the pain but fail, one of the reasons I can never be a submissive. I despise pain and humiliation. *Yet, I did both to Aleah at the first opportunity.* I do not slip into subspace. I simply endure.

Eventually, there's a break in the pattern of pain, and Flare's sharp nails rake down my back through the stinging cuts covering my ass. A hand lifts my chin, and I'm looking into swirling black patterns in purple eyes. "So nice to see you again, Cassiel." She hefts the huge strap-on dildo in the other hand, making sure I see the implement of her torture. This Flare is not the young woman I'd known and loved. Instead, this beautiful fae houses a sex demon with enhanced power.

Flare holds out a hand, and a slave gives her a bottle of lube she uses to coat the dildo. My thanks are short-lived as Flare squirts lube over my ass pucker. It's the warming kind that can cause stinging and irritation and a whole host of discomforts that break the mood, and it burns like hellfire as it hits the cuts on my ass. But at least she gives me the benefit of lube before impaling me.

I barely have time to register that thought when Flare parts my ass cheeks wide and drives the dildo to the hilt, damned near rupturing me in the process. I try to relax muscles rock hard with tension to no avail. She slaps my ass. Hard. Then, she cups my sac and starts to knead. The battle starts between pain and pleasure. Despite her expertise in working my cock and balls, I can't get past the pain riveting through my body. Flare keeps up the torture until uncontrollable tears stream down my face, and my cock is an angry red, dripping semen I can't fully release.

"He won't break, sensei master." Flare's voice reaches me from far away. I go faint with relief when she withdraws the dildo, but it's short-lived as she pounds the dildo up my ass. I call on long-forgotten strategies, and I endure.

"He will. The parasites will do the rest of the work for us." Lord Syrael takes her place, grabs my cock and massages my prostate with expert strokes. "Come for me, little Cassiel, and I'll release you."

I'm exhausted and can't figure out why I'm fighting as pain turns to extreme pleasure. The promise of being set free and a few firm pumps of his hand are all I need to explode out of this nightmare and descend into hell.

3

ALEAH

My heart continues to hop, skip, and jump as part of the happy dance going on since I woke in Troy and Tristan's arms. Something extraordinary and magical connected the three of us for eternity, and whatever the fuck it is feels damned good. I'm filled with as much joy as I had on my wedding day to Troy, and I can't wait to see what this new life brings. *Everything is happening so fast!* My command strength is on the job trying to get me to see reason about this new development. But I feel better than I ever have mentally, physically, and spiritually, and I'm eager to see where this journey takes me.

Earlier, after a lazy breakfast in bed that just happened to be in the room when we woke, my guys bustled me into the large shower and washed me from head to foot. Tristan took my front and Troy my back. Cleanliness led to sexiness, and I had great fun doing a double-duty hand and blow job alternating between the two of them. They rewarded me taking turns fingering, licking, and sucking my breasts and clit until they pushed me to yet another of the all-consuming orgasms that I've been experiencing lately.

Then, as if someone flipped a switch, both men tensed, and the leisurely attitude turned to business. Hands and tongues left my body and returned to making short work of washing and rinsing off.

"What happened?" I ask as Troy heads out of the shower stall, clearly on a mission.

"Not sure, beauty. Nothing to worry about, I'm sure. Looks like Cass pulled one of his stunts at a club last night." Troy winks as he wraps a towel around his waist.

"Yeah, our Cass has been known to push the envelope in scenes sometimes. One of us will probably need to go and tidy up his mess, but it's nothing we haven't done before." Tristan wraps a towel around my torso before toweling himself off. I have to admit I love his attention.

I fully open the connection linking my heart to theirs, but the only thing flowing through to me is love and desire dampened to a low simmer but very much there. I don't get anything on what happened with Cass.

Troy tips my chin up and brushes a kiss across my lips. "Take your time. We'll get lunch together and find out what's going on. Then, we can decide how we want to spend your special day." Troy nods at Tristan before heading out the door. "Don't get lost, you two."

Tristan and I exchange smiles at the hidden message behind Troy's words—I need you near, so don't take long. Tristan's kiss is much longer, much deeper as we again use our bodies to continue the delightful exploration of our new love. Finally, when we're both breathless, he steps back with a sigh. I hug myself at the sudden loss of his warmth. He gives me that smile that makes my lady bits squirt and sing.

"Don't be long." Tristan follows Troy into the bedroom. After my skincare, I take a moment to look at the wide-eyed woman looking back at me. My dark eyes sparkle with joy, and my full lips are plump, giving me that well-fucked look.

A white-blue dust mists the air and clouds the mirror, and I swipe at it before realizing the dust is coming from my skin. I'd attributed the pulsing sensation in my system to a very long orgasmic afterglow, but maybe it's more than that. Maybe, it's the power that everyone keeps talking about.

I walk into the dressing room and decide to see if I can direct my magic with my mind the way I'd done when rescuing Tommy. Maybe that was a fluke. I try to make the hangers move. There's probably some incantation for that and everything else under the sun, but I'll have to wing it. One thing I know for sure from watching a whack of epic fantasy movies is that spells rhyme.

"Slide the hangers one by one. Help me pick the winning one." Cheesy, but it works, and the hangers start moving along the rack slowly. *Awesome!* Since I have no idea what we'll be doing today…I push aside the nagging intrusive voice reminding me I have work to do…I decide to dress casually, in layers. I choose a tan cashmere shell with jeans and ankle boots completing the look with a khaki bomber jacket. I give a quick once over and nod in approval. I'll do.

The murmur of voices stills as I approach the kitchen. Raphael, Tristan, Troy, and Nye look at me as I walk up to the butcher's block. Troy slides a latté my way as they all quietly examine me as if I'm another species or something.

"What?" I ask. My voice breaks whatever spell they're under. Raphael picks up a platter of food and glides over to the table. Tristan moves beside me and squeezes my shoulders.

Nye looks positively delighted as she floats over to hover near me. "We were just talking about you."

"No shit, sherlock. My ears are burning up." I give her a grin to take any sting from the words. There's simply no sting in this gal today. I'm still riding the crest of orgasmic bliss, and the heat flooding through my link with Tristan tells me that another wave is coming in the not-too-distant future.

"Nye's been giving us shit for not being romantic enough," Tristan chuckles.

Nye snorts. "As I recall, the term was dense, just like a man."

"No shaming," I say automatically. It's my new mantra.

"I'm good with dense," Troy says.

"That's because it excuses you from something. So, what are you trying to dodge this time?" I laugh.

Troy isn't bothered in the least. Instead, he grins back at me. "More of this romantic stuff Nye's talking about. And you bet your ass I'm dodging. Something amazing happened between us last night, and I need time to process it. Igniting our bond or whatever the hell happened opened a flood of emotions and random thoughts from you and Tristan. And something's changed with my power." He squeezes the back of my neck, picks up his coffee and moves over to the table, where he takes a seat. Tristan and I follow, and I sit beside Troy.

"Same here, but I have the strong need to do my processing with you." Tristan sits on the other side of me. "That's where you came in. Nye doesn't think I'm romantic enough."

"Methinks Nye wants to get into your pants." I grin up at her. "So far, I'm finding him plenty romantic."

"Yes, well, you have set the bar low," Nye grumbles. Troy raises an eyebrow but says nothing as he passes a platter.

I look around the table. "Isn't anyone going to address the elephants in the room?"

"Yes, Domina," Raphael says. "My thoughts exactly." The man moves so silently I almost forget he's here. "Something has shifted in the omniverse because of your union."

Nye gives what can only be a lascivious grin, and heat

rushes to my ears. Could they *see* us last night? I clear my throat. "Were you watching?" I glance at Tristan to gauge his reaction to the idea of being watched, but his gaze is fixed on Nye. *He can see her!*

Nye gives another snort and floats around to the other side of the table. "Darling, we didn't need to watch. Anyone can see these men are dizzy with you. When you three fucked, your divine light lit up the sky, and the earth shook."

"It was quite splendid," Raphael says.

"Isn't anyone going to talk about how Tristan can see and hear Nye?" I ask.

Nye gives a long sigh. "That is what we're chinning about, darling woman." She smiles and flicks that chopstick she carries, and I can't help but smile back. "I haven't had this much fun in centuries."

"Where's Cass?" I ask. "What happened?"

There's a pregnant pause as all parties exchange a glance I can't read, then my guys get seriously busy with our lunch. Something shifts inside me as if one of the threads linking me to the guys closes. I make a mental note to ask about how opening and shutting the connection works. Raphael moves over to the butcher's block, and Nye flits around the room. Something's clearly going on.

"He's back," Troy says, "and he's had a night, but he rushed by us without speaking. So, I'll go talk to him and figure out what's going on while you and Tristan spend some time together." Troy finally meets my gaze with his usual intensity, but all I read is joy, love, and a firm belief that Tristan and I need time to cement our bond.

"I need this," Tristan says, reminding me that our connection now works three ways.

Okay. The butterflies in my stomach take flight, and I lick my lips at the thought of what Tristan's *needs* are.

Troy gives a quick nod of satisfaction and sits back, relaxing. Tristan gives me *the* grin.

"Have you got something planned?" I'm not sure why I ask because it's evident he has.

"Oh yes." Tristan runs an index finger around the shell of one of my ears, still heated from my earlier blush. "Do I have plans!"

Every single one of my lady bits clamps down in eager anticipation. Then, a dark shadow passes behind my eyes and the same dread that Lord Syrael's eye causes floods through me. I shudder and try to grab the feeling so I can examine it, but as quickly as it came it's gone. Yet I can't shake the thread of fear it leaves.

4

TRISTAN

A wave of fear from Cass shudders through our triplet link, but I shut it down. Thanks to Troy's insight, I have what might be one chance to build the foundation for a relationship between Ali and me. Although I'm fully aware that I'm now living a love triangle, I must carve out my niche with Ali, one that's just mine and hers. I'd been stupid with her once before and almost lost the chance for love and joy that yawns open before me. I'm not about to do it again. Ali *sees* me. She's shown me that. Now, it's my turn to stop being a selfish bastard and let her know I see her.

"Nye, I am not taking crotchless panties. Trust me on this." Ali's ears and cheeks flame with color, but she leans into her embarrassment. "As sexy as they may be for Tristan, I find them uncomfortable."

"Lingerie flatters your pussy, my dear. Speaking of, do I need to teach you about flattering a man's ego?" Nye presses on with her subject, relentless.

Troy sidles up beside me as Nye argues with Aleah about what sex toys and lingerie she'll need to bring with her on the trip to…"help him get it up and keep it up." I pat my

19

jacket pocket for the tenth time, ensuring my special mating gift for Aleah is still there.

"Keep an eye out," Troy murmurs. "When Aleah's wound tight like this, she's about to melt down. Like she did when you met her. It's her way of coping, she internalizes. She appears calm and strong, but her well is about to overflow, and she'll need you to ground her."

I give my brother an appreciative nod as I rub the heat in my left delt. Something fucking incredible happened last night when our mating bond ignited. I swear our three souls merged because of the heightened awareness I have of Troy and Ali. Ever since this quest to keep her safe started, shit's been happening that's changing me on a cellular level. And when it comes to Ali, that means every neuron in my cock now stands at attention. I need to be alone with this woman to explore.

"I'll take good care of her, and you do your best with him." I give a nod to how difficult dealing with Cass can be.

Troy gives me a grin. "You do your best with her, and I'll take care of Cass. I hope your tank's full, bro. You're going to need it." We both watch Ali pick up an overnight bag, blow a kiss in the direction of Nye's hovering ghost and stroll over.

"Ready?" The smoldering looks she gives me with those large brown eyes makes my cock even harder.

"I am." I shift to adjust my junk and grab the bag from her shoulder.

To the outsider, nothing changes, but a white-hot flare of heat streaks through my cock. Ali stands on tiptoe and slides her arms around Troy's neck. He encircles her waist and pulls her close.

"Be good," he murmurs into her ear.

"Bad is better." Her reply is barely audible but rings through our channel loud and clear. After a deep kiss, Troy steps back and hands Ali to me. Our hands touch, and power surges through the angelic mating brand that's etched into our left shoulders. Raphael opens a portal to the Druid's private tropical island. Shimmering heat, lush foliage and the smell of the ocean greet us. Ali steps up beside him and holds up her palm. Raphael gives her a warm smile.

"You won't be needing cloaking elixir on the island, Domina. As one of the Blackstone Manor properties, it's protected by Druid magic. Therefore, demon Lord Syrael will not be able to locate you while you remain on the island." Raphael gives his head that funny bow reserved for Ali and steps aside.

I take his place and grab Ali's hand. "Shall we?"

She nods. We step through, and the portal snaps shut behind us. Ali takes a deep breath and pivots as much as she can without letting go of my hand.

"Oh, my God, Tristan." She pulls me over to the fishpond. "It's absolutely gorgeous."

"Raphael tells me the pond wraps around the front of the house and has over forty rare tropical fish." I snap my mouth shut before it runs on with details about the property. I've learned the hard way that most women aren't fond of architecture the way I am, so I'm not about to make that mistake again.

Ali tugs my hand and points while breathing out a sigh. "Look, a waterfall. And look at all the plants. It's like a mini-rain forest. I don't know where to look first. Can we go see the house?" Her eyes sparkle with anticipation and curiosity, making my head leap into my heart.

Could her interest be genuine?

"Let's get rid of these clothes and explore." Ali drops my hand and turns toward the house. "Shit." She pivots and faces me again. "Can you open the portal so I can go back for a minute?"

I hide my smile. I've been waiting for this moment.

Closing the distance between us, I get up close and very personal. "What do you need, *mon chou?*"

Ali licks those luscious lips as she looks up at me, and the soft breath brushing my face quickens. She takes a step back. "Suitable clothes." She grabs the corners of her jacket and spreads it open. "As you can see, I didn't dress for the tropics."

I put my hands on her shoulders and pause a moment absorbing the exchange of power and sexual energy that flows from our mating brands and circulates through our systems. The intensity of the sensation almost knocks me on my ass, so I can only imagine how startling it must be for someone unused to having magic flow through them.

"Do you trust me, *mon chou?*" Six words, the answer to which will set the tone for the next forty-eight hours. Ali studies me for a long moment, then gives a slow nod.

"Troy and I... Let me start again. I think it's important for us to have some time alone, just you and me getting to know each other without distraction or interference. I'd like us to treat each other to our favorite fantasies. We can start with yours or mine, your choice. All I ask is that we shut out everything but you and me."

"Can we at least go to the house so I can get rid of this jacket and grab a cold drink before we talk?" Her tone is calm and measured, and I don't need our link to see that she needs time to think.

"Sure thing." I follow her up the path to the house and pull out the cellphone Raphael gave me with an app that controls almost every function in the house. Huge carved wooden doors like those at the manor swing open onto a spacious indoor-outdoor living space.

"Oh my God," Ali breathes as she makes a series of small circles across the marble floor of a large, covered patio. I drop her bag on one of the tables and follow her.

"Is there anything you need to get out of the way before we focus on us?" I ask.

She gives me a wide grin. *I so appreciate you asking.* The thought streams through our mating bond.

"Yup. I need to call my editor, Daisy, and give her an update." She walks to the overnight bag I dropped on the table and pulls out an iPad. "Finally, cell coverage."

"You'll want to make it quick so I can lock down our protection. If Syrael has your IP address, he'll be able to lock onto it given enough time."

"I'll make it quick." Ali touches the tablet several times, then smiles broadly at the screen.

"Ali, is that you? I'm so not happy with you right now, girlfriend." A beautiful blond woman frowns through the screen at Ali.

"Hey, Daisy. How's it going? I'm checking in."

"You need to do more than check-in, Ali. I've been worried sick, and Cyrus Stone's driving me to drink. Where have you been? And where are the articles you promised?" Daisy gives Ali another severe look then softens. "But as long as you're okay, that's all that matters."

"I'm okay, and I'm on my honeymoon."

Shock stuns the beautiful Daisy into silence. Ali starts laughing and pointing. "You should see your face, Dais. It's priceless. Go ahead, you can say it. Say, you're shitting me, right, Aleah?"

The more stunned Daisy looks, the harder Ali laughs. Finally, she waves her hand in the air, and a tissue drops onto her palm. She's so engrossed in the conversation that she doesn't realize she's used magic. It's right about then that I realize Daisy's not staring at Ali; she's staring at me. I've inadvertently been caught by the camera.

"Is that..." Daisy's voice trails off as she watches me pull up a seat beside Ali. The look on her face tells me all I need to know. I've been here before and bought several T-shirts. Daisy thinks I'm the rather famous movie star I'm often mistaken for.

"His name is Tristan." I try not to laugh at the expression on Daisy's face.

"You do know he looks just like—"

5

ALEAH

"You do know he looks just like—" Daisy's face freezes into a stunned expression that's new to me and, for some reason, makes me laugh harder.

"Brad Pitt, I know. It's like my wet dream come true." I grab another tissue from thin air, barely registering that I'm using magic. "And he's all mine. Daisy, meet Tristan, my new husband. Tristan, meet Daisy, my editor and dear friend."

Daisy opens and closes her mouth a couple of times, and I have a tiny moment of guilt over my little white lie. But there isn't a fucking chance in hell that I'm going to share that I'm fucking my dead husband, who happened to be a triplet, oh, and an angel. Images of Daisy frantically calling 911 to report my psychotic break flash through my mind, and I suppress a grin. If she only knew.

I study her sweet face. She worries and wants to grill me for more deets, but her signature positivity wins the battle. Smiling, she raises an imaginary glass in the air and tips it in our direction. "Nice to meet you, Tristan. Congratulations. To both of you. I couldn't be happier for you."

"It's very nice to meet you, too." Tristan's voice is full of warmth, and the heat flooding to Daisy's face tells me she likes Tristan's full-blown charmer mode, complete with his megawatt smile. "Any friend of Ali's is a friend of mine."

Brother. I stifle a hefty eye roll as Daisy's blush deepens from pink to tomato red, showing she's not immune to his charms.

"Why's Cyrus Stone bugging you?" I ask. We've spent long enough drooling over Tristan, not that either of them gives a hoot what I think. Using our bond, I stab him with the sharp blade of my jealousy. He must sense my mood because he moves away from the camera, but the short distance does nothing to change the sexual heat he directs at me. As much as I love Daisy, I need to tie this conversation up so we can get back to what matters: us.

"Cyrus is a control freak. He wants status updates. Have you visited any of the clubs on his list?" Daisy asks.

"We're visiting Pandemonium on Thursday night. I've got the second article drafted, and I need to give details about the club. Has he paid for the first article?" I ask.

"Yes, which is one of the reasons he feels entitled to updates." Daisy sighs. "You missed the vaccine clinic. Have you had your second shot? Our vaccine mandate starts today, so we're setting staff up with a QR code until the passport system opens."

"I got my second shot in June. I'll shoot you a scan. Tell Cyrus I'll have the second piece for him next week." I smile up at Tristan as he places a glass of something cold beside my tablet. He leans down and brushes a kiss across my lips, and the heat transfer between us dampens my panties.

Even Daisy must feel the desire because her eyes widen. "Okay, I'll tell him. I'll let you go, but don't be a stranger. I worry about you." Her frown turns to the radiant smile I treasure. "Now I'll stop being a mother hen. I'm so very happy for you, Ali, and I can't wait to meet your new man in person."

We barely ring off before I'm on my feet, snugly wrapped in Tristan's strong arms. I stiffen for a moment, not sure what to do with this kind of spontaneous affection. With Troy, affection other than a brief kiss is foreplay. At first, I'd taken the lack of physical closeness personally until I'd realized it was one of the ways Troy protected his heart.

I relax against Tristan's chest and enjoy the fluttering in my stomach, signaling excitement and anticipation about this new man of mine. I've got new-love-itis on steroids and a chance to explore the newness for the first time in my life. I'd never had that with Troy; he'd been there since my early teens—the older guy helping me deal with the fallout from the abuse. Our love had grown out of friendship, and I'd held back on expressing my feelings. Now, the universe is giving me a second chance at love in more ways than one.

Tristan's smoky tenor voice sends more moisture coursing through my lady bits. He pulls back a bit and smiles down at me.

"What do you want most right now?" He sends the question through our new mate bond, showing me he's one hundred and ten percent focused on my needs in a way I've never felt from a man before. That sends another squirt of moisture happening between my legs.

"For it to be just us tonight." I try out our new channel in response. Suddenly, a strong current flows through me that I'm starting to recognize as Tristan's magical power. That strange blue mist called grace that leaks from our skin sometimes sprinkles into the air like pixie dust.

"Can you feel what I'm feeling?" Tristan sounds almost in awe as excitement leaps in his eyes. "I know all this is new to you, Ali, but we're sharing power. Feel the exchange of essence."

Tristan drops his arms and steps back, studying me for several beats. The energy exchange reduces to a high simmer. Then he slides his hands up my arms, and our mating brand acts as an accelerant, sending flashes of energy through our bond.

"I've got an idea. Let's use our combined power to cast a charm blocking out the world," Tristan says.

Heat bolts through me as his suggestion sends possibilities flashing through me. If we can block out distractions, maybe we can cast a spell to enhance a fantasy. Tristan's grin grows positively wicked, and I realize he can see the erotic images too.

"How do we start?" My tone drops an octave as the growing heat between us blocks out almost everything else.

"I'm not sure, but I have a theory. We may not need it but let's focus on a concise phrase describing what we want to see happen," I say. "Something like—give us time to focus on us, shut out all but sharing our love and lust."

My mind snaps into analytical overdrive. I can't help it. "Does that mean we won't be able to feel Troy anymore?" I'm not sure I'm ready to give up that connection again, even if only temporarily.

"No, we'll still feel him, but the connection won't distract us unless there's an emergency." Tristan puts a bit more distance between us, giving me the space I need to process. He picks up our drinks and moves over to a seating area on the large, covered patio. After setting our drinks on the coffee table, Tristan sits on a white love seat and stretches a tanned arm along the top. He doesn't say a word, nor is there any sense of pressure or haste coming through our bond, yet I'm pulled to him on a cellular level I want to explore. I don't want to miss this chance.

I, of course, perch cautiously on the edge of the sofa. Every fiber in my being screams to go to this new mate of mine because I know it will please him. And suddenly, submitting to this man becomes a mission in life in a very different way than I have with Troy. It's as if accepting our bond exposed a need I hadn't realized I had. Or one I'd repressed.

But for the first time, maybe ever, I don't want to analyze anything at all. I want to feel, to be with, to please this man.

"Give us time to focus on us, shut out all but sharing our love and lust. Got it. What do we do next?" I'm rewarded with a smile that damned near makes me come on the spot.

Tristan holds up his left hand. The instant we link fingers, grace and energy crackle around us. "We say it together."

And we do. "Give us time to focus on us, shut out all but sharing our love and lust." Something shifts in the atmosphere around us, and suddenly nothing matters but this man.

My heart beats so hard it's frigging near punching out of my chest. I want to kiss him so badly I can barely breathe. But that new feeling takes over, the one telling me to slow down, to let Tristan show me a new way of loving in a way only he can give. His desire is at the boiling point like mine, but it's tempered by something I can't identify that makes me want to ride with him into the volcano.

Tristan traces my face with his fingers as if he's a blind man while his eyes stay locked on mine.

"What do you want?"

I don't know if he breathes it aloud or if the words transmit through our bond because nothing exists but my need to be with him.

"To please you." My words are a breath that should be impossible to hear, but this gorgeous man who is now mine smiles and gives me the best gift.

"I have a fantasy for us. What's our safe word?" Tristan's clever fingers continue to make my lady bits clench, playing with my face and neck while he waits, something I'll need to get used to. But, unlike Troy, Tristan seems to have an eternal well of patience to draw on.

"Socrates." I probably should have said the word we'd all agreed upon before, red. But I have the sudden need to share something that's all our own, although I'm not sure if the source of the feeling is him or me. The continuous flow between us tells me we share so many of the same feelings of wonder and confusion over this newfound bond.

He smiles. "So, you think I'm going to corrupt you, do you?"

He got it in one, and that understanding deepens my desire. "I know you're going to corrupt me." I send a jolt of impatient desire through our link, and he wags his finger in the air.

I huff out a puff of air, but we both know I'm intrigued and can't wait to see what happens next. "So, tell me our fantasy."

6

TRISTAN

My Ali wants to please me. That message flows through our mating connection loud and clear now that we've removed all obstacles to focusing on us. I fight down a smile and the urge to spread Ali's legs wide and take her on the spot. Her impatience insistently pushes at me through our mating bond, but I won't be rushed.

I want to give her something no one else has. Not even her beloved Troy. She yearns to role-play throughout the Double Diary, but Troy never could expose himself enough to take on another role. Likewise, my brother could never be the frontman of a band and would make a lousy actor.

As much as I love Troy, I know his faults. Know there is room for me to make my mark and develop my unique bond with this woman. Troy would have studied her until he found the perfect equation for bringing her maximum pleasure. Once discovered, my brother would rinse and repeat.

"So, tell me our fantasy." Ali's rigid with sexual tension as she perches on the edge of the sofa beside me. I sweep my gaze over her petite body as she bites her lower lip showing every bit of the appreciation I have for her exquisite beauty, inside and out. She blushes and looks at her lap but not before I catch her insecurity warring with delight. It's going to be an uphill battle slaying Ali's doubt armies so she can understand the power she holds over me.

"I think an arranged marriage will be apropos," I say. "As I recall, you're a fan of royal period pieces."

Her brown eyes sparkle with delight as she claps her hands together. *"Yes, please."* She says nothing, but the words sing in my mind loudly and clearly.

"So, I'm Prince Tristan of the Blue Vale realm, and you're Princess Aleah. My power and position, along with your pedigree and lands. Your husband, my older brother, bankrupted our kingdom and left you with a huge debt. The evil barbarian he owed seized you and put you up for auction when your husband died under questionable circumstances. I bought the lands and your hand. You need my power and protection. If you leave, the barbarian will kill you. I have the reputation of being a ruthless dominating bastard who takes what he wants when he wants it."

"So, you're rich and powerful and a demanding prick. We barely know each other because you were estranged from your brother. I didn't want to but had no choice but to go through with the wedding. The ceremony is over, and you've brought me to this island to make sure I understand my role as your wife and submissive. A taming of the shrew, so to speak." Ali sits forward and touches my arm.

I love how she jumps right in and adds to the story. My cock goes rock hard as her desire sears through me, desire heightened by her curious mind. "Let's say I've taken possession of your belongings, including your diaries."

She nods. "Is there anyone else on the island with us?" She licks her lips, and those dark eyes stay glued to mine. I take a moment to read the emotions swirling through our mate channel. On the surface, her heart hammers, and her rational mind screams, *"not in this lifetime."* But beneath her inhibition simmers a yearning I want to expose and explore. But tonight's not for sharing. Tonight is for us, my Ali and me. Our connection tells me that need runs just as deep within her.

I nod slowly and am gratified as she hugs herself and shivers. Should this person be a man or woman? Or both? Best to start slowly. I have so much to learn about this Aleah. "There's one other person here with us, my housekeeper, Sadie. She'll be serving us tonight."

Ali says nothing as she studies my face, and the intensity of her desire sends tingling through all my extremities. Time to get started.

"Safeword, *mon chou?* Hard limits?"

"Socrates. No hard limits. I trust you. Let's see where our desires take us. It kind of takes away from the idea of being forced if I can safeword out."

Her trust and openness melt my heart and make me even harder. I don't know whether she sees my long-buried desire to play with taboo scenarios or whether she needs the freedom to explore some taboos of her own. Whatever the reason, it's something we can do together.

"Shall we begin?"

Ali nods then clenches her fists and squeezes her eyes shut. Finally, after three or four beats, she sighs and opens her eyes.

I stroke her face. Every pore in me screams with the need to touch my newfound love, to stay connected with her. "What's the matter?"

She shrugs. "I can't figure out how to shut down my busy brain so I can stay in the role." She frowns, then brightens. "Can you help, Tris? Use your power to put me into the role for tonight?"

My breath catches at the way she says my name as if

whispering her love through the breeze. "I can." I lean forward and brush a kiss across her lips, keeping our bodies a hair's breadth apart. "Although we can use our power with the strength of our minds, I find it helps me if I articulate my wish in words. Ready?"

Ali nods eagerly. I cup her cheek and murmur the charm.

> *For the next twenty-four hours, you will be,*
> *Princess Aleah, who's been sold to me.*
> *A royal prince of the realm with powers divine,*
> *I own your ass and will make it mine.*

Ali closes her eyes as our grace swirls around us. Suddenly, her posture goes rigid, and her eyes spring open. She looks at me and startles as if she'd forgotten herself for a moment, then she scooches away until several inches separate us. Then, she narrows her eyes at me and clears her throat.

"Let's get one thing straight, Prince Tristan. This is a marriage of convenience, plain and simple. There will be no consummation of this marriage, period. There is one reason and one reason only I agreed to marry you. You are my husband's brother and will treat me with respect. This is a business arrangement. You chose to marry me to solidify your hold on *my* lands. These are *my* people, and they will not give their loyalty to you without my influence. That and to keep my pedigree in the family." She keeps her small body rigid with personal power, something I find sexy as hell. The charm's done its work, and she's fully immersed in the role of hard-done-by widow.

Feisty. I like it. Even though it's a role-play, my memory manipulation spell brings out Ali's authentic self.

"I chose you because you're special. I married you because

you're hot. Your lineage and position are simply icing on the cake. You have no reason to doubt me."

"No? Let me see, where do I start?" She raises her index finger. "You're white. You're male. You're rich. You're powerful. I'm black, female, damned near destitute and clearly without power. I know you only want me for one thing, a taste of dark meat. A taste you will *never* get. Does that answer your question?"

"Enough." I slam my fist on the table with more emphasis than force, but it's enough to make her jump. "Let's get one thing straight, milady. Under English common law, a marriage contract gives me certain rights, and the right to fuck any one of your orifices is one of the gods-given rights." I draw back and pick up my goblet, toying with the stem. "However, I've never been one to force myself on a woman. The only thing I require from you is honesty."

She averts her gaze.

"Look at me." I put some snap in my voice, and she responds immediately. Goosebumps appear over her skin and the dark streaks in her eyes light up. Good.

"What is the one thing I require of you?"

Our eyes do battle until the word finally passes her lips. "Honesty."

I wait.

Ali takes a deep breath. "I give you my word."

"Good. And you have my solemn oath I won't do anything without your consent, milady. However, one way or the other, I'm getting fucked, but perhaps you'd rather watch?" I raise my voice a notch, gratified by the quickening in Ali's desire. "Sadie, come in, please."

A beautiful Armenian woman wearing a long white sheath strolls from the house's interior and kneels before us. Raphael wasn't kidding when he said the island comes complete with a fully trained submissive. I rise, slowly and deliberately, tip Sadie's chin and study her. Hair so black it's almost violet reflects off eyes the clear blue of a summer sky, and her full lips beg to be kissed. I let Ali fidget for several beats before turning slowly and looking at her, drawing out this teasing torture. "Pretty, isn't she?"

The Princess Aleah pretends she hasn't been watching us intently by studying her wine before looking up at me. "She's okay." She shrugs again, but she can't keep the tightness from her tone or hide the lust flowing through our mate bond. Desire emanates from her in waves, urging me on. I do hide a smile as I ramp up the attention I pay Sadie. Let's get my little Ali dripping wet.

"That's a little disingenuous, don't you think, milady?" I infuse a false mildness into my tone then look at the submissive. "Would you like to fuck me, Sadie?"

"Yes, sir. I'd like that very much, sir," the lovely Sadie says. I couldn't have asked for a more perfect sub to play the role.

The Princess Aleah makes a choking noise.

"Or perhaps the Princess Aleah would rather you fuck her?"

7

ALEAH

It feels like another reality exists somewhere way off in the distance, but I can't bring it to mind. I'm the Princess Aleah forced into marriage with my dead husband's evil brother. A brother I've secretly lusted after for years, although I barely know the man. A lust I'd never let see the light of day but helped busy my fingers as I lay alone in my bed at night.

Now, here he is telling me he owns me, but no man will own me ever again. At least the bastard says he won't force himself on me. I glare at him and the woman he's ogling. He doesn't seem in the least bit inhibited.

"Or perhaps the Princess Aleah would rather you fuck her?" Tristan asks Sadie the question, but his tone makes it clear it's a statement. He's giving me three choices—fuck him, watch him fuck her or let her fuck me while he watches. I wet my lips again, unable to stop the nervous habit as I try to figure out whether I'm mad as hell or intrigued.

I've been around enough powerful men to know a mind game when I see one. This fucker's lain down his cards and is calling my bluff. I study Prince Tristan's face for any sign of weakness, but the man radiates as much strength as his brother did, if not more. I bite my bottom lip as I deliberate and try not to look at the woman. I gave my word I'd be honest. I need time to think, so I say nothing.

"Ah, she's thinking." Prince Tristan looks at Sadie again. "What's your safe word, little one?"

No fucking way!

"Freyja, sir." Sadie gives the name of the Norse goddess of love. Prince Tristan takes his time raking his gaze over her body. My agitation ratchets up at each inch of her he explores, and I swear I can hear his voice in my head.

"At another time in another life, this sub would have topped my list of playmates, but no more. Realization hits me in a pleasant way. I have no desire for this woman, beautiful and delightfully submissive though she may be. I want to sink balls deep into you, Princess Aleah, and stay there for a lifetime. But I want more than anything else to satisfy your deepest desires, and if that takes fucking the lovely Sadie, I can take one for the team."

I frown as his thoughts stream through our mate bond. I make a show of taking a sip of my wine before sending my reply loud and clear through our bond. *"I don't share."*

"Ah, so you want her to fuck you?" The prince sprawls back on the love seat beside me and stares me down as if he doesn't want to miss any nuance that lights my eyes. What does he see? Confusion? Curiosity? Definitely desire.

"Strip, Sadie." Prince Tristan issues the command, but I feel his eyes on me.

I watch Sadie like a hawk.

Sadie rises and slowly pulls the long white sheath over her head, revealing a deeply tanned, curvy naked body. She sinks back to her knees, head bowed.

"Come closer and show your mistress that lovely body," Prince Tristan commands. Sadie moves closer to us, and I do my best not to shrink into the love seat.

"No, thank you," I say. "I'm not into women." But the

rapid pulse of my desire threatens to expose my hidden fantasies.

"Ah, so my new wife insists on fibbing despite agreeing to be honest. I'm getting a little tired of your attitude. Do not speak unless I ask you a direct question. For the remainder of the night, every word you speak without permission will get you one stroke. Do you understand?" Prince Tristan grabs my chin, forcing me to look at him. There's no mistaking the coldness in his gaze; he means business, and something in me responds to that bite. I fight the desire to submit.

"Yes, I understand." I glower at him to hide the clenching of my lady bits at his mention of punishment.

"Sadie, expose." Prince Tristan gestures at the floor with his index and middle fingers. My eyes seem glued on the woman as she sinks to the floor, knees spread, hands locked behind her head, eyes down.

"Good girl." Approval laces Prince Tristan's tone, but he's looking at her, not me.

"Now, let's try this again, Princess Aleah. Would you like Sadie to fuck you?" Prince Tristan asks.

I say nothing. Technically he has given me permission since he asked a direct question, but the bitch goddess in me refuses to comply so easily. Besides, the pause gives me time to think. I might like to try a taste with a woman but only to see what it's like.

"Answer me!" He has that snap in his tone that makes me want to drop to my knees.

"No, I do not want Sadie to fuck me tonight." I hold my breath hoping he doesn't pick up on the nuance. No such luck.

"Fair enough. Tomorrow then for fucking," the bastard says. He must decide to test my limits because he pushes the coffee table out of the way. Tristan points his thumb and index finger at the floor, and the woman crawls toward us. "A taste then. Sadie."

I share equal measures of horror at the thought and longing to take her place. As she moves all sinuous and sexy, Prince Tristan brushes my breast through the soft knit of the shell I'm wearing. Again, I shiver. I'm dripping wet, and I can't take my eyes off this Sadie, more specifically, her generous breasts.

"Would you like to touch them?" Prince Tristan asks.

His question shocks me back to reality, and I remember myself and whip my head around to glare at him. I'm the Princess Aleah. I will submit to no man. "No, I would not like to touch them. What I would like is for Sadie to do her job and get us something to eat."

Prince Tristan opens his mouth, no doubt to call me on my lie, but I derail him. I give Sadie a pointed look. "Now!"

"As you wish, mistress." Sadie rises, gathers her dress and pads from the room with a distinct fanny wiggle.

As the door closes behind Sadie, I release a long breath before downing the rest of my wine.

"You want her," Prince Tristan says.

"Any moron can see she's beautiful. But that doesn't make me want to have sex with her," I snap.

His royal highness arches an eyebrow, letting me know I'm not fooling him with my protests.

"So, I get to fuck you." Prince Tristan takes another sip of whatever the hell he's drinking while I glower at him. But my treacherous body is busy begging for this man to sink his cock into me.

"Fine. Let's get it over with. Where do you want to do it? Here?" I gesture to the love seat. "There?" I fling an arm toward the wall, but I'm wound so tight the gesture seems hesitant.

"Sixteen strokes so far." The man looks as if he can't wait

to get me over his knee. "Admit it. You want me. You've always wanted me." His stern tone lets me know he has zero tolerance for evasion.

"Fuck you." I put an equal amount of bite into my tone. Something in me wants to push him. Wants to make him strong-arm me into submission. Wants him to take me over his knee and spank me until I'm begging him to make me come. As soon as the thought lands, I try to snatch it back.

"Eighteen." The satisfied gleam in his beautiful blue eyes tells me it's too late. "Take off your clothes."

Thankfully, Sadie chooses that moment to come back with a large tray laden with dishes. And she's still naked. Damn. I open my mouth to tell her to get dressed and clamp it shut again at Prince Tristan's warning glance.

"You'll be happy to know Sadie is a very talented lady's maid. Sadie, help your mistress undress."

My mouth opens and shuts a few times of its own accord, but I'm too busy swimming against the upstream of my desire for anything logical to come out. She reaches for me. My arm lashes out. I snatch it back when it lands between her breasts and then stride over to the table. I turn and give Sadie a wonderfully fake smile as I take a seat.

"Thank you, Sadie. We'll ring if we need you." I grab the cutlery, uncover a dish, and dig in, making it clear I'm not interested. If only my traitorous libido would agree.

8

TRISTAN

Something akin to bliss unfurls in me as I watch Princess Aleah struggle with her desire for kink. I have no idea what possessed me to test her limits with another person, but I can't ignore the urge to follow my instincts.

I take my time, sitting across from Aleah on the covered patio and preparing to eat the light meal Sadie prepared. Another bolt of desire travels through me as I watch her make a big show of being unaffected by Sadie...and by me. But the energy flowing between us lets me know it's precisely the opposite. I've awakened a curiosity in my little Ali that she's never allowed herself to explore, which makes me wonder what else there is to uncover.

"Eat," I command.

Despite her efforts to appear nonchalant, Ali keeps throwing furtive glances my way. I hide a smile and let her stew for a few minutes while I eat the light meal I requested. I'm a grazer by nature and prefer not to play on a full stomach. Nevertheless, the steak salad with a creamy vinaigrette Sadie made hits the spot. When I'm done, I slowly cross my knife over my fork and slide the plate to the center of the table. The Princess Aleah has given up all pretext of eating and intersperses stares with sighs making it clear she's not waiting patiently.

I meet her hot gaze. "I see you're still dressed. When I give an order, I expect you to follow it to the letter."

Princess Aleah does the fish-lips thing again before snapping her jaw shut like a trap. The next instant, her right hand shoots into the air. I hide another grin. "You may speak."

"I never agreed to be shared. If you want me to play by your rules, you'll need to be fair about it." She sits back, clasps her hands in her lap and gives her head a sharp nod.

I raise my eyebrow, loving the thrill that runs through our mating bond. "Never fear, milady. If I share you, it will be because you want it."

She presses her lips together, and it takes several long beats for her to rise, ever so slowly. Finally, after a frantic look around, she removes her clothes and takes a stance with arms akimbo to show her defiance. I stand and slowly walk around the table until I'm standing a few inches behind her. She shivers again as I brush the curls from her right ear.

"I will not tolerate defiance, Princess A. You can play princess of the manor with everyone else but me. With me, you will remember at all times that I'm your lord and master. You are mine, bought and paid for, and I expect unconditional obedience." I keep my voice pitched low, making the words a wisp of breath drifting past her ear and am rewarded as a ripple of heat makes her tremble.

But she remains rigid, and that arm shoots into the air again. I want to laugh, but instead, I grab her shoulders and turn her. "Speak."

She hugs herself, but her heated gaze remains defiant as she faces me down. "Before we proceed, I want to know the terms of this deal. How long will it take me to pay off my husband's debt?"

I trace a finger under the soft swell of her small breasts. "Let's see. Five million dollars. If we're going to monetize this, that depends on just how much each fuck is worth? Will you be a willing or unwilling participant?"

Another shiver, but she holds the glare. "What difference will that make?" She shifts as I trace the dark brown areola encircling one of her nipples. Another almost imperceptible quiver washes through her.

I go rock hard and fight the urge to bend her over the nearby love seat and fuck her into oblivion. Instead, I cross my arms. She rewards me with a hint of pink as her tongue flicks to her lips, then looks around again nervously.

"What are you looking for?" I ask. A good Dom is always aware of the nuances of his submissive and explores what they mean.

She looks toward the ocean again. "We're outside."

"We are." I wet my finger and resume circling her now pebble-hard nipples.

"We aren't going to do it out here, are we? Where everyone can see us?"

"Are you bothered because we're outside or because someone might see us?" I assume it's the latter. I know from the diaries that Ali and Troy have played around with light BDSM, but my brother isn't one for a public display.

"Both."

"Good. Let's hope this is the first of many things I'll introduce you to while you pay off your debt. What's your safe word, milady?"

She glares at me. "First, we finalize the terms of this little deal. How long before I'm free?"

As I stare down the challenge in those dark eyes, I'm thrilled to see that my Ali's fully immersed in her role. I'm having more fun than I've had in several centuries. For the first time in a very long time, I feel alive and eager to see what tomorrow will bring with this magnificent woman.

"Five years is more than generous." I hold up my hand as she opens her mouth to argue. "Five years as my submissive. During that time, you will meet my sexual needs with cheerful readiness. Once the terms are met, if you wish to go, we'll divide the territory and any proceeds we've made during the term fifty-fifty. I think that's more than fair."

Princess Aleah looks thoughtful then nods. "Agreed, but I want it in writing."

I find a pad and pen behind the bar, scribble out the terms and slide the paper to her. She keeps her arms over her breasts as she reads and crowds against the bar to sign the paper. Body image shame looks the same no matter the species, and I make it another one of my missions to help Ali see the same beauty that I do. She straightens after signing and gives me a now-what look.

"Let's get your punishment out of the way, shall we?" I add the bite of command that turns her crank as I move over to a chaise lounge and take a seat and drop a cushion on the slate patio stone. "Over my knee."

She hesitates, then huffs but makes quick work of settling over my knee.

"Safeword?" I put the flat of my hand on her back, relishing the heat radiating from her.

"Socrates. What's yours, by the way?" She's topping from the bottom, but she's right to ask, so I let it pass.

"Persephone."

Ali gives a quick skeptical nod of recognition at my choice. "Don't expect me to spend one second more than five years in your company no matter what I eat."

"Understood." I run my right hand over her round ass before sliding my left palm under her left breast. "Twenty-seven strokes." My hand itches to strike and grab her firm globes now that they're mine.

"Oh hell, why not make it an even thirty, *sir*" She puts heavy emphasis on the word, so there's no doubting her sarcasm, and wiggles on my lap. Based on her earlier reactions, I expected resistance to taking her over my knee. Instead, I'm reading simmering anticipation and need.

"Ah, so you did learn something about being submissive from the lovely Sadie. Now, count." I deliver the first stroke on the lower half of her right ass cheek while I squeeze her breast. Ali gasps and arches back from the shock of the sharp strike but settles back a hair before the second slap hits her right cheek.

"I said count." Slap.

"Three." Ali bites out the sound between gritted teeth but remains still.

After ten swift strokes to warm her ass, I press each cheek firmly where the crease meets the ass and am rewarded by the involuntary contractions of her gluts. Although spanking can cause the similar ass clenching women use in auto-erotic play to reach orgasm, Ali proves to be hyper-receptive, squeezing her ass in rhythm with my strokes.

I take stock to monitor the color of her skin and check for bruising. Her ass is a dusty rose that enhances her tawny complexion. Despite the contractions, Ali's muscles are relaxed, and she's extremely excited. In centuries as a sex angel, I've spanked and fucked many females, but none of them were as sexually responsive to spanking as Ali. And it took less than ten strokes.

Ali moans, bringing me out of my reverie. *Slap.* I resume spanking increasing the force with each slap now that she's warmed up. The more blood that rushes to her pussy, the more excited she becomes. By the time we hit thirty strikes, she's pushing her ass into my hand. Her legs part almost involuntarily. Her moans are low and guttural as I do another check-in. When I pinch her nipple and slide a hand between her wet thighs, her pussy clenches around my fingers.

I pull her quivering form into my lap and hold onto her with fingers drenched by her essence.

"Now tell me you don't want this, milady. Soon, you'll be begging me to fuck you. Hell, getting you dripping wet took no time at all." I bait her to see if she's still engaged in the scene.

Straightening her spine, she leans her face close to mine, letting her hot breath wash over me. "You may be able to elicit a reaction from my body, but I will never beg you, Prince Tristan. Never. I will not enjoy this." Her voice is husky and raw with yearning.

"I accept your challenge."

9

ALEAH

"Please don't enjoy this. I'll enjoy taking you enough for both of us." The bastard gives me a long look while I try not to wiggle my naked stinging ass in his lap. It takes me a moment to realize I'm panting as I look down into my brother-in-law-turned-husband's hot gaze. The staccato of my heartbeat and blood rushing in my ears drowns out any sound as he grabs a handful of curls and yanks my head back. Something about that spanking changed me. Makes me crave more. It should have hurt, but it didn't. Instead, the stinging quickly became a warm current of euphoric desire flowing through my system. For a second, I wonder if this is the subspace I've read about. But the thought drifts away before it can take hold.

"Before dawn breaks, you will beg me to make you come." He rakes his tongue and teeth across my breasts, none too gently, making my stomach clench with need. "But you will not come until I say you can."

"Fuck you," I grunt out. And suddenly, I'm overcome with the urge to have my new husband take me like a caveman

48

from behind. To continue making my ass sing while he fucks me. Hard.

"You have quite the saucy mouth on you, milady. That just earned you another spanking." He drives two fingers into my cunt and taps my G-spot. The stirring in my lady bits signals an orgasm is bubbling to the surface, but he removes the fingers and sets me on my feet before it takes hold.

My skin is so sensitized that the ocean breeze hitting my skin at the removal of Prince Tristan's heat is almost painful. He points to the armless chaise lounge we just left then removes his clothes. The curved chaise is made of memory foam that is the perfect length and width to accommodate me. I move to stand next to the top of the chair without taking my eyes off his gorgeous body. I get a brief glimpse at his very large cock before he stalks over and pushes my chest over the chair. Next, he kicks my legs apart, opening my sex, putting my lady bits and ass on full display.

"So pretty." His naked body brushes mine as he whispers in my ear before sliding his hand through my wet folds. Another involuntary moan escapes. I thrust back as my clit desperately seeks his magic touch.

Several more slaps to my tingling ass submerge me in that feeling of relaxed euphoria. Then, by adjusting my stance, Prince Tristan puts space between my thighs and the chaise. He drives into my drenched vagina without warning, adding rocket fuel to my desire. I moan as he pauses, balls deep, and my core clenches spasmodically around him.

He leans over me again, and his hot breath on the back of my neck pushes my heat meter up another notch. "Like that, do you, milady?" Prince Tristan circles my folds with his hand, lightly brushing my clit with each pass.

I push into his hand, using my body to say the words I can't. *Rub my clit. Make me come.*

The prince shifts and clamps a hand on my left hip, anchoring me in place.

"Uh, uh, little one. Tonight is my night, my rules. You know what to do when you want to come. You'll have to work for it." He takes a few long, slow strokes that torture my G-spot while he uses those wicked fingers to tease my clit. I use my upper body to push against his hold, but I can't budge him. With each stroke, my nipples brush across the top of the chair, sending shards of lust through me.

He chuckles and rubs the pad of his finger over my painfully engorged clit. "Do you like it when I rub your clit like this?" The fucker sounds as calm and relaxed as the still water in a reflecting pool while I sound like a braying mule. And right now, even that sounds hot. I moan but say nothing. Prince Tristan gives my ass a hard slap bringing forth another moan as waves of pleasure cascade through me. Nothing exists but my need for this man and the pleasure he can give me.

But I'm almost over-charged. Nothing matters but coming. Gone is the lady of the manor trying to assert her power. I moan again as I try to press into him. He stills but holds me rigid, all movement stilled.

"Do you like it when I rub your clit?" He enunciates each word slowly and carefully, oblivious to my efforts to rub against him. I want to rock against his hand, rub my clit until the fire building in it explodes into the universe.

"Please, your highness." I pant. I beg. I can't help myself.

He slaps my ass again hard. "Tell me what you want?"

I hate talking during sex, and no men ever asked what I want. Royal princesses are taught to do their duty—spread your legs and pray it doesn't take long. If one wants good sex, one takes a lover.

Slap. Fuck, that feels good. So does the push and pull of wanting to fight and submit to this man.

What do I want? A yawning pit opens inside me, letting out every dirty little secret I've ever had. I want him to fuck me every slippery, sloppy way possible. I want him to make me come and come and come until I drop from exhaustion. I want...

"I want you to rub my clit until I come," I gasp out.

He lets out a low moan of his own and returns two fingers to my clit and rubs, still balls deep in my cunt. As my orgasm starts to build again, I try to buck against him. He holds me fast, and fuck, it's sexy.

"Is that all you want?" he growls in my ear.

I don't want to speak. I don't. I don't.

"Milady." His command undoes me.

"Fuck me, sir. Please, sir. Hard." I barely get the words out before Prince Tristan pistons his hips into mine, his fingers keeping perfect rhythm on my clit.

For one delicious, brilliant second, I stand pitched forward at the edge of a very high cliff. Prince Tristan pinches my bursting bud and I shatter into a million pieces, scattering on the wind. Then, with a roar, the prince joins me.

I barely have time to think or recover, when this man flips me so that I'm sitting on the lower edge of the curved chaise with his face between my legs. He spreads my engorged lips and inhales deeply.

"Gods, how I love your scent." His tongue feels deliciously rough as it rakes across my folds. He takes three long licks before fastening his mouth over my engorged bud. Two long fingers slide into my pussy and tap on my G-spot. "This pussy is mine now."

I groan and rear up as another orgasm springboards off the receding aftershocks. Prince Tristan makes no bones about his love for my pussy. He sucks and licks, and finger fucks me until his face is coated with our mingled cum and I'm shaking from exertion.

After he has his fill drinking my pussy, he flips us around, pulls me onto his hard cock and cups my breasts.

"Show me what you want." His voice is hoarse with need, and his cock pulses in my cunt, but he doesn't move. At that moment, any remaining cares and fears leak away, exposing the desperate secret I've hidden for so long. I want to try rougher sex.

I look down into the smoky blue eyes challenging me. This prince is my new husband. Although the details are fuzzy, that much feels real. What happens here tonight will set the tone for the rest of our marriage.

"Make me," I hiss out.

In the blink of an eye, I'm on a bed with my wrists and ankles cuffed to a wedge pillow with bars that raises my ass into the air, completely exposing my wet cunt. The mattress dips with Tristan's weight as he crawls between my spread legs, all the while fisting his cock. My mouth waters in anticipation of tasting that cock when the prince grips the sides of my throat and moves my head until I have no choice but to look directly into those searing eyes.

My breath catches, but then I realize it's desire, not fear, flickering through me. Prince Tristan tightens his hold slightly, not enough to impede my airway, but by God, there's no doubt I'm in his power.

10

TRISTAN

My heart sings as I look down at the woman sleeping curled up against me. Like Troy, I've been obsessed with Ali from the day we met all those years ago in the forest. But Troy had needed her fierce protection, and I'd put my feelings on the back burner. I'd convinced myself that knowing my brother had found some measure of peace was all that I'd needed.

That deception had worked wonderfully well until I'd seen her again, and this time, as a grown woman. Then, even from across the room, a glimpse of her stole my breath away, and there was no denying the current that passed between us the moment we touched.

Never in a thousand years had I considered the idea of multiple mates. Nor would I have considered my brothers and me to be one of few blessed with a divine mating bond. But it makes sense with our little one. Ali is one of those women for whom sex both provides fuel and release to blossom, and she's more than capable of handling the shit three dominant men will throw at her.

I brush a mess of curls behind her ear, uncovering her flawless light brown skin. Ali's expressive face can go from resting bitch face to a radiant angel in less than a split second, but at the moment, she's at peace. A peace I'd helped her find.

"Thank you." Ali's eyes remain closed, but her voice rings strong and true.

"For?" I send my question through our mate bond.

She opens those brilliant brown eyes and smiles up at me before poking me in the chest with her pointer finger. *"Don't do the obtuse thing with me, buster. You know bloody well what for."*

A delighted laugh bursts forth before I can catch it. Ali sees me, and she's letting me know it. "You're welcome. Anytime. Like now." I cover her small frame with mine and explore her mouth as if it's a new archaeological find that needs handling with great care. But our persistent desire fuels the force of our kiss, and we only come up for air when we're panting.

I pull her against my chest, and we lay quietly, enjoying the heat of each other's bodies while we catch our breath. I'm almost drifting off when my beloved rustles.

"Time for a bio break." Ali sits up and throws off the sheet covering us. "Then, I'd better find us something to eat."

I prop the pillows and lean back, so I have a better view of her pert ass as she walks toward the bathroom.

"No need, babe." I hesitate for a split second, but I decide to go with my gut. "Sadie will bring us what we need."

Ali's about to disappear into the bathroom, but that brings her to a dead stop. She pivots, walks to my side of the bed, and studies my face. "Do you want to fuck her?"

I can't get a read on her feelings through our mate bond. She raises her eyebrows as I probe, letting me know she's aware I'm there, and she's not letting me in. *"This is about you, not about me."*

Another thrill goes straight to my cock at her insight.

There's no hiding with her. I grab Ali's hand, and arousal instantly flows through our mate bond.

"No, I don't want to fuck Sadie. I want to fuck you until you're too weak to walk, then I want to fuck you again. I want to fuck you every way you'll let me, and if that involves fucking Sadie, I'll take one for the team."

My fierce lover snatches her hand out of mine and punches me on my right bicep. "You'll take one for the team, my ass. Hell will freeze over before I ever approve of a scene that involves you fucking Sadie or anybody else. Are we clear?"

"Crystal." I nod, but her jealousy tickles the devil in me, and I can't help but give a little nudge. "Does the same apply to a scene that involves Sadie fucking you?"

Ali goes stock still for a moment, no doubt recalling last night. She stares at me, through me, for several long moments before releasing a long sigh. "It might. Go ahead. Call Sadie. I want hot tea with honey and lemon, please." Without another word, she sashays that sweet ass out of sight.

Last night, I'd taken a gamble by using sex to help Ali release the stress of constant change and living under a death threat, and I'd won the jackpot. Now that our mating bond is fully open, she can't hide the toll the stress takes on her despite her casual attitude. But, although she's one hell of a lot more at peace this morning, there's still work to be done. I clap my hands twice to activate the automated intercom system.

Sadie's voice filters through hidden speakers, low and sultry. "Good afternoon, sir. How may I be of service?"

"Please bring us a breakfast tray and include a pot of tea with honey and lemon for your mistress." I keep my tone neutral and stress the moniker so that Sadie's very clear on where things stand in the light of day.

"I'll send it up in the lazy waiter in five minutes." Sadie's voice fades as the system cuts off. Raphael and Nye seem to have kept their promise of ensuring our every whim is met on this short honeymoon of sorts.

I get up and pull on a pair of boxer shorts before pressing the button labeled "Wake." Immediately, the blackout shades open on the windows and skylights, and the large sliding doors open, revealing a dining nook on a large wraparound deck. The climate-controlled wood floors are on the cool side as the morning sun slides into the full heat of the tropical afternoon.

When I hear the lazy waiter, I retrieve a loaded tray and spread the bounty on the intimate table overlooking the Caribbean Sea. I grab a cup of coffee and lean my elbows on the deck overlooking a large, landscaped back yard and pool. Using my Guardian mode, I scan the area for any sign of Lord Syrael or weak spots in the security. Despite Raphael's assurance that the island is protected by Druid magic, I feel better being vigilant.

I pass Ali a mug of tea as she sidles up beside me and touches my arm. Our bond acts like a magnet, pulling us together, and the instant our skin connects, magic and sexual current flows between us. The bond breaks for a few seconds as she leans away and picks up her mug to take a sip. I can't stand the separation. She sighs as I grab the back of her neck, reminding me that the same hand grasped the side of her neck last night, exciting us both.

After several minutes, Ali sits down and helps herself to fresh fruit, a croissant, and a selection of cheeses. I join her and take the lid from a steaming bowl of oatmeal and raisins. After adding a splash of steamed milk from a small carafe, I sit back and observe my beloved. Our connection lets me know she's got something that she needs to get off her mind. *Do you see me?* The thought is barely a whisper as it drifts through our mating bond, but it echoes through my mind. Do I see her?

She attacks her food with gusto as if she's fortifying her walls, but I realize she's probably refilling the well. I'm content to let Ali take the lead on our next steps. When I understood that my Ali could release her stress through sex instead of tears or a panic attack, I worked her until we both dropped from exhaustion. We both need nourishment, especially given my plans for the day ahead. But first, I need her to let go of whatever she's hanging onto.

Unlike Cass, the hum of her internal computer doesn't threaten me. After scarfing down a large bowl of oatmeal and a couple of eggs, I wait until Ali's ready. When she finally finishes fussing with her food and trains her gaze on my face, I lean forward and take her hand.

"Talk to me." I let our connection do the rest of my talking and let our bond show her that I'm not either of my brothers. That I can be here for her without trying to fix things for her or change her.

Ali squeezes my hand, and a flash of hope flickers through our bond. She quickly releases my hand as if she feels it and the connection's too much for her.

"You and I have no rules set for us in our relationship. Everything's new. It's a fresh start. We can be authentic with who we are. When we hit the bumps, we'll figure them out. I've never had that chance with Troy because… so yes, I'm pretty fucking happy about having the chance." Ali stares at me intently as she probes and prods our bond looking for what? I give her my most supportive smile and wait for her to continue.

Me too. Where the hell is she going with this?

"I can't shake the feeling that something is very wrong with Cass, that he's going to hurt me. Maybe badly. Or betray me. I know I'm new to all this magic stuff, but I don't think

I'm imagining this." She twists her hands as if she's pissed at herself for not figuring it out.

I take her hand so she can feel the *knowing* behind my words. "You're not imagining anything, *mon chou*. You probably have the gift of precognition. Our souls see it in each other. Ignore those messages at your peril. Forewarned is forearmed. What do you want to do about it?"

11

ALEAH

When Tristan takes my hand, there's no denying the magic flowing between us. But there's something different that wasn't there before. It's more than the certainty, the *knowing* I've had since our mating bond ignited.

"What do you want to do about it?" Tristan doesn't try to convince me I'm wrong, and the current flowing between us confirms my fears. Except it's more than fear hitting me about what's coming with Cass. Something dark hovers, a dark shadow in the corner that's getting harder and harder to ignore.

"That's what I need to figure out." I squeeze his hand, letting him know how much I appreciate and need his unconditional support.

Tristan gets up and flashes *the* smile at me as he pulls me to my feet. Rubbing my arms as if it pains him to break contact and with eyes that radiate with love he says, "Let's get you dressed. Then how about we finish the tour that got so wonderfully interrupted last night?" His kiss sears my lips before he spins me and slaps my ass. The low-slung boxer shorts do nothing to hide his muscular ass as he struts off.

I follow him into the luxurious bedroom and take a look around. Tristan had used his magic to alter my memory so that I became the Princess Aleah to his Prince Tristan in our fantasy, so decor hadn't been a priority at the time. Everything about the room screams Tristan, and I can't help but smile and hug myself as another piece of knowing him drops into place.

He turns and gifts me with the smile. "What? I can feel you thinking about me?" He waggles his eyebrows.

Heat rushes to my ears, yet I can't help but laugh. "It wasn't *that*. I was thinking about how this room speaks to your tastes in architecture."

Tristan pulls me into his chest and runs his fingers through the slickness between my legs. "Oh really? Architecture, eh?"

Laughing, I slap at him again, dodge around him and into the walk-in closet I'd found earlier. Rows of clothes and lingerie hang on two walls. Floor-to-ceiling wooden cubes line the third wall stuffed with folded garments. Like the Manor wardrobe, every piece is my size and color palette, as Tristan had them custom-made for me. I'm about to throw on shorts when a short sleeveless black silk dress snags my attention. It's cut low under the arms and will barely cover my ass. Holding it against me, I look in the wall mirror. It's a lot racier than anything I'd usually wear, but that was before I was the Chosen, had not one but two husbands and am about to venture down kink county lane. After all, we're alone here or almost at any rate.

I push aside the image of Sadie kneeling on the floor, refusing to be distracted. Tonight is my time with Tristan, and I'm no longer the kid who grew into love with Troy. Instead, I'm a forty-year-old woman with a hot new husband who craves my mind and body, and he's not shy about showing it. I drop the chemise dress over my head and consider going without undies for a nanosecond. But some habits die hard, and walking around with juices flowing down my thighs doesn't appeal, so I opt for a thong. Finally, I slide into a pair of sandals and grab a visor.

Tristan wolf-whistles as I join him in the bedroom. He's wearing a light linen T-shirt that hugs every muscle and baggy drawstring pants that make my hands itch to loosen.

Grabbing my hand, he takes me on a tour of the splendor around us, and I'm mesmerized by the depth of knowledge he has about architecture. I let his excitement and joy roll over me as he proudly points out handcrafted custom beams with mitered edges, limestone heated floors and all manner of luxury conveniences. He's like a guy in a smut store, excited and animated as he pulls me through the house.

The kitchen is splendid and something I'm comfortable chatting about. It's a cook's kitchen, and I ooh and ahh over the massive gas range with dual ovens and Japanese ash cabinetry.

"You'll love this room." Tristan opens the door to a beautiful library that leads into a perfect home office.

"I love all the wood." I run my hand over one of the built-in shelves.

"Isn't it great? That's mahogany." After a few minutes showing off the electronic windows and blinds, Tristan presses a button, and the floor-to-ceiling windows slide into corner beams. He continues the tour into the indoor-outdoor dining room and center courtyard where we'd scened last night. Heat flashes through me as I remember my naked body bent over the chaise lounge, legs splayed wide—

"Earth to Aleah." He takes me across a large grass area, pointing out stables and Sadie's quarters. I stifle the need to ask about Sadie and follow him through some dense foliage into a clearing with a sparkling waterfall and pool. A large stone fireplace is built into the landscape beside the waterfall, with comfy upholstered lounge chairs scattered around a coffee table. Tristan sits on a couch and pulls me down beside him. He pours a large glass of what looks like cranberry cocktail over ice and hands it to me before pouring his own. Electricity pops between us as our fingers brush.

He studies me quietly and intently while he drinks. Being devoured like this is a new feeling and not entirely comfortable, but I lean into it, letting his current flow through me. But before I can get my fill, he puts our glasses on the table and pulls me so that I'm sitting with my back to his chest, his thighs imprisoning me in place against his hard-on. He wants me. "Not yet, *mon chou*," he says.

"Now that you've had time to think, any idea about how we heal Cass?" I ask. "What if I can't save him?"

"You will, and we'll have your back."

That he treats me as a partner and takes ownership in this fight makes my pussy pulse. God, I love this man. But business first. I shiver as I turn my thoughts to the shadow that grows at the edges of my mind.

"So, you feel it too?" I let the heat of his arms cloaking mine comfort me for a moment. Then, the shadows part on Cass raping my battered and bruised body.

I gasp as the essence of Cass's feral ferocity flows into me. The pain is so intense I turn in my mind to flee. Tristan's body holds me fast. "Let it in, Ali. I'm here with you. We can handle it together. Find your way past the pain. Feel my light." Tristan's voice sounds far away, but that feeling deep inside makes me respond to the command in his voice.

I feel my way blindly through the darkness in my mind until I see a tendril of Tristan's essence. I grab it and hang on. The instant the threads bind, our grace brightens and swirls around like pixie dust absorbing the darkness and changing it to light. It's the same thing I did with the dark magic at the Manor. The pain recedes as Tristan's power combines with mine, and in our vision, he shows me how to channel the light.

I'm panting hard and shuddering when we break the connection. Tristan wraps me tighter in his arms and sends his healing essence to soothe my raw edges. I can't escape the dark magic in the vision as it lashes and batters my divine light. Nausea builds as I feel the searing pain tearing at every cell in my body.

"I don't know if I can do this," I whimper.

"I'm with you. Try again." He pulls me back into the vision and helps me face the demons time and time again. With each try, our combined power grows stronger and consumes more of the dark magic.

The sun's setting, and we're starving and drenched in sweat by the time Tristan's satisfied with our progress. We drain tall glasses of cold water before he strips out of his clothes and heads toward the pool. Despite the lights reflecting from the bottom of the pool, it's almost impossible to see Tristan as he disappears into the inky water. Not being a swimmer, I sit on the stone lining the large pool and enjoy the warm tropical night air as it cools my hot skin.

I startle when he pops up beside me, brushing wet blond hair from his eyes before placing a large hand on my thigh. "Ready for our night?"

I turn an equally hot gaze on my man. No doubt that's a euphemism for probing my kink limits. His eyes hold the weight of probing questions I'm not quite ready to explore, so I change the subject.

"Out of curiosity, why aren't you trying to talk me out of me putting myself in danger?" I gesture toward the star-filled night sky as if that might define the "this" in the equation. Although I might not know what's coming, I can't shake the feeling that I'll need to sacrifice myself to save my guys. How much do Tristan and Troy know about what's coming?

He shrugs those gorgeous shoulders. "What would be the point? The universe set us on this path. Who am I to question it? You know what you're doing. That's why you're chosen."

TRISTAN

It's a mystical, almost spiritual experience working with Ali to use her power and as much a learning experience for me as it is for her. One would think I'd have had my fill of touching her after almost constant physical contact for almost twenty-four hours. Yet the moment I surface beside her, and put a hand on her thigh to renew the connection, my cock goes rock hard. I resist the urge to scramble out of the pool and flip her on all fours. To fuck her on the spot and do what a good Dom should…attend to her needs.

Her dark eyes sparkle with intensity as she looks down at me, looking for answers only the Megaverse can give and seeing something I can't read. But it's clear as fucking glass she's looking for something more than my somewhat fatalistic outlook on my motives. I wait for the inevitable scathing comment when she realizes I have nothing profound to say. Meeting her gaze, I wait for her disappointment to ride the current of our mating bond. I hold my breath waiting for the pain of her rejection. There's no doubt that the intellectual bond between Troy and Ali is a fundamental part of the cement that bonds them. Troy would have had something profound to say.

"Stop that!" The sharp edge in Ali's tone cuts through my self-pity. After a penetrating look, she drops her gaze to my hand and traces lines on the back of it.

"You're very different, and I don't know what to do with that." A tropical breeze catches her whisper, but I could swear I hear you're different *from your brother* echo in the wind.

She stands, and the wet edges of her short dress cling to her ass as she grabs a beach towel from a chair. I pull myself out of the pool as she walks back, holding the towel high. Standing on tiptoes, Ali wraps the towel around my shoulders before pulling my head down for a deep kiss. Gripping her beautiful round ass, I hoist her up and set her on the back of a nearby chair. I push her dress up then return to grabbing her fine ass. She digs her heels into my ass and pulls me tight against her body. Nothing separates us but a wisp of a G-strap.

Her tongue dances over mine with a silent song written for me. *"At this moment, at this time, I need you. Not Troy. You, Tristan. Body, mind, and soul."*

As she kisses me, her grace calls to mine, pulling it forth until it binds with hers to form a new cord. Only then does she break the kiss.

Taking a huge breath, she pulls her head back and laughs. "What am I going to do with you? I should take you over my knee, mister." She pokes her right index finger into my chest. "And never doubt me again, or I just might."

"Oh yeah? You and what army?" I grab her wrists and pull her arms around her back.

She laughs up at me. "Now, you do remind me of your brother." Then she pushes me and swivels around to sit while I catch my balance and wrap the towel around my waist.

"I want to try something." She pushes a button on a remote sitting on the coffee table, which I'd shown her earlier, and a large screen drops into view. Picking her up, I settle her onto my lap and pull her back against me.

"What are we looking at?" I adjust my hips taking pressure off my hard-on as she wiggles in my lap.

"Give me a minute." She sits perfectly still, barely breathing for several long beats. I make use of the time by using my fingers to explore the perfection of her petite body.

"Get your ass over here, mister." Ali's smoky voice projects through hidden speakers. My larger frame dwarfs Ali's as my bare ass bends over her legs. "Pause."

The action on the screen stills. Ali wriggles around in my lap until she's looking at me with earnest eyes that sparkle with mischief. I get the distinct feeling that she's dipping her toe in waters no one's ever allowed her to sample. Helping my Ali explore her power and affinity for kink is a gift I hadn't counted on, and her none-too-gentle reminder makes me go rock hard. I slide a hand up her side and pinch a plump nipple.

"Are you making a movie, *mon chou*?" I keep tracing the soft flesh of her breasts as I wait for her response.

"Yes," she breathes, and the perfume of her arousal filters into the air.

"I'm pretty sure they say cut, not pause."

"Well, I'm directing this movie, and I wanted to pause." She waves her hand, and screen Ali tries to spank my doppelgänger but can't balance his large body on her lap. I laugh as Ali's movie turns into a series of Tristan slapstick falling pranks that have me laughing my ass off.

"Pause." This time, a woman moves into view on the screen wearing nothing but a short maid's apron. Although we can't see her face, there's no doubt the woman presenting Ali with a tray of flogging implements is Sadie. I chuckle and am rewarded with a glare, and Sadie disappears from the screen. Ali sticks her tongue at me before turning back to the screen.

The movie continues with Ali examining and discarding several toys before settling on a paddle with fur on one side and suede on the other. By this time, I'm on all fours. Ali struts around me, smacking the paddle against her hand.

"Cut. May I make a suggestion?"

"If you must," Ali huffs out.

"Use a spanking bench for your first flogging. It'll give you better control."

"I'm not flogging. I'm *spanking*." Ali emphasizes the last word as if I'm a moron for not understanding.

"What's in your hand?" I toss back the ball.

Ali rolls her eyes dramatically, still wiggling in my lap, well aware of the effect her hot ass has on my package. "A paddle. Duh." Mirth trickles through our bond, and her delight is an aphrodisiac. I'm the one lightening her load, helping her prepare for what lies ahead. Screen Ali slaps the paddle against her thigh for emphasis. "Ow," she says.

I grin, letting her know I'm thoroughly enjoying the show.

"A paddle means it's a flogging. If you want to spank, you use bare hands." I marvel at how little my little angel knows about kink. Although Troy's memories as a sex angel were blocked, I would have thought it part of his DNA. Maybe she's a switch. Something we hadn't considered. "Have you never spanked or flogged someone?"

My question wipes the smile from her face and brings her back to our reality. The screen goes dark. She turns her entire focus to my face but says nothing. Finally, she says, "Once, sort of."

I'm about to ask her to explain when I realize why the universe revealed her gift for visualization. "Show me." I put the edge of command into my voice. The screen lights up, and I'm pleased by her immediate response.

The image of Troy appears, standing naked with hands bound above his head. Ali walks around him, dragging a flogger with medium falls over his skin. I study Ali's doppelgänger intently as she starts flogging. She takes a few tentative swipes, and it's evident she's uncomfortable. Yet, here she is, bringing up the subject with me.

When the scene ends, I ask, "Did you like flogging him?"

"No, but I wanted to see how it feels to be the one in charge." She grips her hands tightly in her lap but continues to meet my gaze. Again, I've stumbled into an area of vulnerability, and I need to gauge my reactions carefully.

"And did you like being in charge?" I keep my voice gentle, nonjudgmental. She shakes her head.

But you want to spank me?"

Again, she shakes her head, and I stifle my frustration. It's my job as a Dom to get past her inhibitions, to help her discover her inner kinkster. So, we sit silently while I give her the time she needs to work through her layers of guilt and shame.

Finally, she releases a long sigh and says, "I don't want to spank you. I thought it might be stimulating to watch someone spank you, that's all."

So she's a voyeur like Troy? "You like to watch?"

"Not really."

Through our bond, I send a taste of disapproval, letting her know I expect more and am gifted with another of her sighs.

"I like to watch smut movies if they're well done. They're a great way to set the mood."

"Do you like watching scenes at the clubs?"

She nods slowly. "Yes, but I think they're more performance art than authentic. What I'd like to see is how people respond when they don't know they're being watched." She wiggles again, warming up to her subject. "I would love to see a real sex scene with a real orgasm and without all the fake panting and moaning." She gives her head a sharp nod followed by a shake. "Oh well, pipe dreams." She starts to wiggle off my lap. "Let's go get something to eat. I'm starved."

I hold her fast and wait until I'm sure I have her attention. "Tonight, I'll show you a real sex scene with a few real orgasms, but there will be panting and moaning. The real kind."

A myriad of feelings flicker through our bond—fear, desire, guilt, need, but it's her intense curiosity that spurs me on. I grab Ali's hand and head back toward the house. I'll make our last night alone together one we'll remember for a very long time.

13

TRISTAN

We're back at the house and crossing the indoor-outdoor dining area when Ali goes rigid. Panic shoots through me, although I'm not sure how much of it is hers versus mine. I grab her arms, trying to get a read on what's wrong. Suddenly, I'm inundated with glimpses of the vision that's locked Ali in its hold. I see Cass pushing Ali to her knees before a man dressed in black leather, Ali unconscious hanging from a modified St. Andrew's Cross, and Cass whipping Ali's bloodied back. Then, as Ali drops to her knees, my precognition kicks in, and I see the leather-clad man smiling down on Cass as he grips his arms precisely the same way I'm holding Ali and says, "Well done, my boy." Or at least that's what I think he said. The image comes and goes so fast it's hard to tell.

I drop to my knees and gather Ali while I try to sort out what the fuck happened. Our hearts hammer in overdrive, and it takes a minute to realize my system is reacting to Ali's. The bond shows she's in a full-fledged panic attack, trembling and almost hyperventilating.

It's not sex she needs right now. It's comfort. Gathering her in my arms, I run her through the mansion to the master quarters. She's having one of the worst panic attacks I've ever witnessed. By the time I drop into a large stuffed armchair and wrap her in my arms, she's shaking uncontrollably, and hot flashes and abdominal cramps flood through her system. Holding her tight and rocking, I bathe her with healing essence and pray to the gods to loosen their hold on this woman.

"I've got you, babe." I want so badly to shut down our connection, so I'll stop feeling her pain. Instead, I grit my teeth and use all of my power to widen the channel. A wave of dizziness hits hard, followed by a paralyzing tingling, numbness. *Oh god. Oh god. Make it stop.* Her mind stutters through several options and lands on one. *Breathe. In-two-three-four. Hold-two-three-four.*

Slowly and steadily, she wrestles her panic under a semblance of control as crippling head pain slams in. I wallow in a well of helplessness before Nye's voice breaks into my head, loud and intrusive. *"Think, you ninny. You are a healer. Heal!"*

"I can only heal damage connected to or through sexuality. This isn't." But her thought gets me thinking. I'd healed Ali with kissing and the exchange of sexual essence. Each time, I'd felt a pull as if I could take on her pain like an empath. Empathic healing is rare, and few are willing to take on the pain of another, but I don't hesitate. With this woman, I will walk into the fire.

I adjust our bodies so that her face tips up toward mine and send tendrils of healing power through our bond. The intensity of her pain takes my breath away, but her vulnerability and love are like a hook, drawing me on. I smooth the curls from her face and whisper in her ear, "I've got you, *mon chou.*" Then, I open my power and pull her pain within. I'm limp with fatigue by the time I absorb and use my magic to obliterate the symptoms. Ali rests quietly in my arms. I tip my head back and close my eyes for just a minute. We have so little time left, and I want to experience so much more with this woman.

When I startle awake, it's full night, and it takes me a second to get my bearings. Ambient light from outside and the lit gas fireplace provide enough illumination for me to see Ali's observant eyes regarding me. She flattens a hand on my chest, and healing love floods through me as she smiles up at me. Raw hunger for this woman replaces all traces of our earlier pain and fatigue. She responds through our connection in kind and bites her bottom lip. A peek at the tip of her dark pink tongue gives me an instant cock stand.

Ali's fingers dance between my nipples, but the move isn't sexual. The shadow in the background has moved closer, and she has something to say. With a sigh, she sits up, turns in my lap, and locks her hands loosely around the back of my neck. She gives me a sad smile.

"I wish we had more time." She leans her forehead on mine for several heartbeats before leaning back and watching me intently. "This link between us is fucking amazing, and now we know our power flows both ways." Ali holds her hand in the air rotating her wrist releasing a mist of grace that surges into me.

I, too, wish we had more time. Time to admire how quickly she assimilates information. Time to appreciate her courage and humor. But I won't waste a moment of now wishing for what isn't. Instead, I raise my hand and mimic her action. "Agreed."

She shifts in my lap until she straddles me and then consumes me with those hot lips. My tongue rises to the challenge as she plunders my mouth and our tongues begin a fencing match that soon leaves us breathless. She breaks first and leaps off my lap, agitated. I still and watch for clues. What does she need?

"I need a drink. You?" True to form, my Ali tells me. She crosses to a whiskey decanter and ice bucket sitting on a table, picks up a glass and tips it at me. I nod. I rarely drink, but tonight I'll make this small exception. Ali pours several fingers in two glasses and hands one to me before crossing to the deck. I join her, and we drink silently, gazing at the lush tropical resort-style courtyard. A wave of sadness washes through our connection, but I resist the urge to pull her into my arms. That's not what she needs. She needs this separation to get through what she needs to say.

Finally, she clears her throat. "You saw. Lord Syrael is close. He's like a presence that hasn't gone away since our mating bond."

I purse my lips. Should I tell Ali I saw something too? That my brother betrays her? Betrays us all? The bastard. I'll kill him for this. I tense and force myself to relax. Confronting Cass will wait, assuming Troy doesn't beat me to it. He's probably already figured out what Cass is up to. But Ali needs me here and now. I set our glasses on the deck before turning her and looking deep into those dark eyes. I cup her cheeks. *I've got you.*

She reaches up and returns the gesture. Then, several too short moments later, she turns back to her drink, gazing into the darkness. "I have a strong sense that Lord Syrael got to Cass." She hesitates a moment, grips her glass tightly then continues. "The demon lord has some kind of hold over him from your childhood. It isn't very clear. I get images that look like the ones Tommy showed me, and I'm not sure what belongs to whom. But there's something there."

Shock and clarity hit me simultaneously with full force. Images from the dark years after losing our parents when Lord Syrael took Cass away for hours after telling us how lucky we were to have a big brother to look out for us. Of Cass crawling into bed in the wee hours of the morning, crying and bleeding. Of Cass curling into a tight ball and refusing to let me or Troy comfort him. So many emotions hit me I don't know what I'm dealing with, but Ali's warm touch grounds me, brings me back to what I need to do. She gives me a tiny smile of understanding before looking back at the horizon.

"Cass needs me to save him. You and Troy need to save each other so all three of you can save me." My brave Ali bows her head, heavy with the weight of her upcoming burden.

"What do you need?"

She throws me another glance of gratitude. "I need you to help Troy forgive Cass. I need *you* to forgive Cass. I can't shake the feeling that if you three aren't united, aren't bonded, then I'm doomed." She says this with such finality, I shiver. Although it will be a struggle, I'll find a way to forgive Cass and move on, but there's no fucking way Troy will ever forgive Cass if he hurts Aleah. But I don't have time to dwell on that now.

"If you need us, we'll be there." I say it with assurance and finality I don't feel, but one thing I know for sure, I will die before I lose Aleah now that I've found her.

"Where there's a will, there's a way." She takes the words out of my mouth. Gods, this woman is amazing. But there's something else stirring in our mating bond.

"What else do you need?"

"To be Prince Tristan and Princess Aleah for one more night. Both of us in the role and let the chips fall where they may." She's working mighty hard to control her breathing, but I can't miss her underlying excitement.

"We can do that." I walk over to the mantel and pick up the box I'd hidden earlier. "But first, I have something for you."

14

TRISTAN

I'm sitting in the back seat of a limo beside my new husband, more than a little drunk and horny. Prince Tristan has been silent during the ride home from the Masquerade, an elite sex club for the rich and infamous where he'd strutted me around to stake his claim. Although my memory of the evening of sin and iniquity is hazy, I do remember one thing quite clearly…letting one of my husband's rivals touch me against his express command…while he watched.

It wasn't my fault that I'd run into the naughty Duke Nicholas, one of the nobles who's been trying to get between my legs since my cad of a husband got himself killed. And, I didn't *ask* him to run his wandering fingers down my bare spine damned near into the crack of my ass.

Power and testosterone leak from my new husband as he sits beside me in the limo with his powerful thighs spread. I don't need the dim running lights to know that those blue eyes are trained on me, no doubt contemplating the punishment I know is coming. Or waiting for me to apologize. Well, it's time this man learns a few things about me, and first is that I will be subservient to no man.

Before we'd left for the club, my prince had made it very clear what tonight was all about. I knew the rules, and I'd broken them anyway. A delicious shiver runs through me as the limo pulls up to the mansion that marks the seat of Prince Tristan's territory. His housekeeper Sadie's duties seem to include chief driver and submissive. When she opens the rear door, Tristan exits the car and strides into the house. Gone are tonight's earlier niceties when he'd played the courting gentleman to perfection. Back is the belligerent bastard who thinks he owns a piece of my ass.

Sadie opens my door looking like a knockout in a sexy chauffeur's suit. Although she bows her pretty head in submission, there's nothing meek about the voice that hisses at me. "You'd better get your ass moving, mistress. You don't want to make him any angrier." She rakes her eyes over my scantily clad body, sending heat rushing to too many parts of mine. "Or maybe you do."

I'm too flustered to think of any retort, so I take her soft hand and let her help me from the car. "Thank you," I manage before I flee up the walk after my husband's disappearing back.

The man looks fifty shades of delectable in a dark gray Vagabond overshirt tucked into steel-gray Zante pants that mold his ass perfectly. Black Cardinal shoes complete the outfit, subtle in understated elegance on the body of a powerful predator. Prince Tristan stalks through his mansion and climbs the stairs that lead to his bedroom.

My heart takes an undefined leap as he marches past the sleeping quarters to throws open a door. I stop short in the doorway and try to get my intoxicated brain to identify what I'm seeing. Exercise equipment? My brow furrows in confusion. Why does the prince want to exercise? I mean, really? We've just been watching kink galore. Exercise is definitely not what I have in mind.

"It may not be what you have in mind, but I'll certainly get a workout." The prince scowls at me, although I could swear I see a flash of humor in his eyes before they go cold. "And those had better be the last words out of your mouth unless I ask you a question."

I snap my traitorous mouth shut as my ass tightens. Last night's spanking hadn't hurt at the time, but I could still feel the after-effects. As I look into the candlelit room at three pieces of equipment, my ass clenches again. A closer look at the piece on the left makes one thing very clear—it's a bondage board. Beside it sits a cross between a chair and a GYN exam table. The Kama Sutra chair I'd been sprawled over last night sits off to one side. I swallow and hustle my butt into the room at the look on the prince's face.

Prince Tristan points a finger to a spot in front of the board, and I cross to it, trying desperately not to let my nervousness show and desperately wishing the wisp of cloth he'd allowed me to wear as undies weren't drenched.

The bastard makes a great show of removing his over-shirt to show his muscular chest clad in a very fitted dark gray T-shirt. I can't help myself; I lick my lips and try not to breathe as he moves behind me. When he runs his hands lightly down my bare arms, I can't hide my shiver. "Is that a flashlight in your pocket, or are you just happy to see me?" My voice is husky as I murder Mae West's famous line, but I don't care. If it kills me, I'll make this man react.

"That's fifteen strokes." Now he trails his finger down the same path Duke Nicholas took earlier, and I skip a couple of breaths. "Now, how many stokes should we give you for deliberately disobeying me?" His voice is conversational as his hands slip under the black satin covering my breasts. When I don't answer, he pinches my nipples hard, and another bolt of molten heat shoots through me.

"I asked you a question." His voice is deep and deadly

quiet in my ear and should make me very afraid. This new husband's reputation for brutality is legendary.

"Ten." I manage to get the word out despite my suddenly dry mouth.

He grabs a handful of curls and yanks my head back hard. "Ten, what?"

"Ten, sir." Another delicious shudder rolls through me as I choke the words out.

Without another word, he yanks the sleeves from my shoulder and shoves the shirred skirt over my ass until it drops to the floor. He lifts my arms above my head and places them on the handles on each side of the padded blackboard. After adjusting the height of the board to his satisfaction, he kicks my feet apart, something I'm coming to recognize as a signature move with him, and one I find hot as hell.

I try to slow my heart rate and convince myself I'm not on the verge of a panic attack or another of the best orgasms of my life, whichever comes first. Meanwhile, Prince Tristan makes a show of choosing the implement of his torture. Finally, he settles on something that resembles a leather spoon. My eyes damned near pop out of my head as he tests it against his palm, inches from my face.

"Safeword?"

"Socrates." The word's barely out of my mouth when he starts beating on my ass and thighs. Those twenty-five stripes answer any questions I had about being a pain junkie. I'm getting damned close to calling my safeword when the bastard stops. He grabs my sore ass with one hand and my chin with the other and studies my tear-streaked face. Sheer determination keeps me from making a sound while he whips me, but I can't stop the tears falling from my face.

He cups my mound and hisses, "This cunt belongs to me, milady. I and I alone will decide if it's to be shared.

"Yes, sir."

"Yes, sir, what?" His tone remains cold, but there's a subtle undertone of heat that wasn't there before.

"Yes, sir. My cunt belongs to you." The words slip out easier than expected as the heat continues to build between my legs. He slips two fingers into my wet heat then slides my juices through the crack of my ass. My legs start to tremble with need as my anticipation builds. Surely, he'll take me now.

But this man is disciplined. He steps back and points to the chair beside us. I sit as demurely as possible while I watch his muscles move in perfect rhythm as he takes off his clothes. He's only a few feet in front of me when he drops his pants. His magnificent erection springs free and aims directly for my mouth, all huge, hard, and engorged with his need. But before I can react, he has me trussed up and spread eagle in the chair.

He lowers his bulk on a stool between my legs and pulls a suspended tray filled with an array of sex toys within reach, never taking his eyes from mine.

"And now, milady, let's have a look at this hot little cunt of yours." He adjusts the chair, bringing my open pussy to mouth level.

After sliding the pads of his thumbs through the slickness in my folds, he uses them to spread my engorged lips wide. Then, leaning forward until his nose is a hair from my clit, he breathes deeply. My pussy clenches, and I strain forward, trying to reach those lips that are so close yet so far, but his fingers hold my spread thighs firmly in place. The sweet agony of his hot breath on my cunt forces my knees farther apart.

He sits like this, studying my spread pussy but only touching it with his breath until I'm almost out of my mind with desire. "Now, let's see who this dirty little cunt belongs to."

Only then does he take the tip of his mouth and trace it around a clit so engorged it's painful. My body spasms as he teases my clit, never entirely giving direct contact but centering every ounce of blood in my body to that one spot until I'm sweating with need. But all I can do is writhe and moan and try to hang on why it's so important not to submit to this man's hot mouth.

I'm ready to give anything for *la petite mort* when the seeds of an orgasm start to sprout deep within my core. Prince Tristan's tongue taps my clit before he trails it lightly over it. Wash, rinse, repeat. Sensation grips every cell in my body as an orgasm steals free.

"Who owns your cunt?" His words only add fuel to the violent contractions that have taken hold of my pussy.

"You do, your highness." My voice is ragged and broken, but I no longer care. Nothing exists outside of this man and this moment.

"That's right." He drives three fingers into my cunt, adjusting them until they're hitting my G-spot. "Only in here, I'm your lord and master."

"Yes, master." I'm not sure if the words make it past my moans as another orgasm builds on the crest of the last.

When he pulls out of me, I'm panting and sweaty, and I've never felt more beautiful or alive. Quivers run through me as the aftershocks dissipate. When I finally open my eyes, both the man and his cock are standing proudly before me. Prince Tristan tips his head back and takes several long pulls from a bottle of water, exposing a long neck made for me to rake my teeth over. God, how I want to touch this man. My fingers flex reflexively as the candlelight hits the dark blond dusting of hair that trails from his chest to his navel. Suddenly, I want that body to be mine.

My eyes bulge wide as he lifts a purple butt plug from the tray beside him. Taking his time, he squirts a generous amount of lube over the toy ensuring every square inch is covered. He adjusts the angle of the chair, giving greater access to my anus. Another quiver rockets through me as he slowly inserts the tip into my opening. My anus clamps shut at the intrusion. Prince Tristan gives me a penetrating look as he nudges the plug a little deeper. "First time?"

I nod frantically and try to relax into the taboo sensation. The prince gives a small, satisfied smile, then leans forward and sucks one of my hard nipples between his teeth. His sharp bite sends darts of delicious agony straight to my lady bits, causing me to relax my sphincter. Then, the prince buries the butt plug. A new sensation fills me as his long thick cock slides into me. With each thrust, the prince's cock hits a sweet spot deep within my vagina that's stimulated by the butt plug.

There's nothing to do but close my eyes and let pleasure sweep through me like fire until the blazing flames consume me. Consume us both.

I'm limp and languid as I slowly slide out of the fantasy. After releasing me from the restraints, Tristan puts his over-shirt on me and pulls me into his lap on the Kama Sutra Chair, cuddling me until my trembling subsides. The strong current of his love flows through our bond as our divine essence combines, strengthening our power. Making us more together than we can ever be apart.

"I have something for you. My mating gift for my warrior woman." Tristan motions, and a square blue box flies into his open hand. At the last minute, I remember I'm forty years old, and I stop from clapping in glee as he hands me the gift. I flash this man, who I'm so desperately attracted to, a for-me smile before lifting the lid. A carved gold cylinder lies in a nest of black tissue paper. I lift it eagerly, examining the runes carved into the metal.

Tristan covers my hand and says, "Dagger." A blade of light springs from the blade glimmering in the dim light.

"Is this?" I twist in Tristan's lap, damned near neutering him in the process. He laughs as he adjusts my ass over his junk.

"A light dagger, yes. It's made using ancient Druid magic, and you can use it to stun your enemies with lust or set it to kill. It will respond to your commands and wishes." Tristan cups my face and leans toward me, intent on holding back reality for a few minutes longer.

A sudden crackling noise ruptures our moment as a portal to a padded room yawns open beside us.

"What the fuck?" Tristan tightens his arms around me as he leaps to his feet, wings extended. A foggy black aura whirls around Cass as he steps through the portal and snatches me out of Tristan's arms.

"This is for your own good, baby brother." Cass gives an evil laugh as the portal slams shut behind us. Eyes dark with madness send terror rushing through me as he manacles my wrists and attaches them to a thick chain hanging from the wall.

"Now, you're mine."

I almost choke on terror as darkness closes around me.

Upon ascension to Bardo, Atroyel almost destroyed the examiners in his grief and rage, knowing Black Rose was vulnerable to Syrael's attack. The chief justice took pity on him and allowed his prince brothers to anchor his disembodied spirit to the Earth realm. She gave them the power to shield Black Rose but advised that only the exchange of divine grace shared in true love could break the spell binding Black Rose to Earth. They must not try to convince or coerce Black Rose in any way, or she'd be lost to them forever. The princes were overjoyed with the opportunity, praying it would give them the time they needed for Black Rose to recognize and accept their love before Syrael found her.

Now, there was just one problem. No longer hidden by Troy's magic, Black Rose's face appeared in Lord Syrael's magic mirror, alerting him to her presence on Earth. The princes had no time to lose if they were going to save Black Rose from the horrific fate the dark lord had planned for her...

Because this time when he'd stepped in front of the magic mirror and said, "Magic mirror on the wall, who is the most powerful sex angel of all?" the mirror announced in a rather smug voice that Black Rose remains the most powerful sex angel of all."

When Lord Syrael heard the mirror saying this, he shook with self-righteous anger. "Black Rose will die," he shouted, "if it costs me my life."

Then he went into his most secret dungeon where no one else has ever set foot where he made a deadly poison chocolate-dipped strawberry. He carefully dipped one-half in the poison milk chocolate and the other half in white chocolate. If Black Rose swallowed even a tiny piece of it, she would die.

But unbeknownst to Lord Syrael, the Oracle had foreseen his threats to the Chosen and cast a spell redirecting her soul to the Void where she would gain power until the forces of eternal and everlasting love broke Lord Syrael's hold. Only then would the Chosen assume the full power and authority of a Transcendent Nephilim. Once ascended, she shall lead an army of sex angel lords to eradicate all forms of sexual abuse from the megaverse.

15

CASSIEL

The moment Sex Demon Lord Syrael laid hands on me, things became crystal clear. The Megaverse may have chosen Aleah, but all that exotic beauty hides her true evil nature. She has to be destroyed once and for all, but that's for Lord Syrael to do. My job is to break her and deliver her to him. No matter how much I hate the thought.

Turns out, Lord Syrael had possessed the media magnate, Cyrus Stone. Within nanoseconds in Stone's presence, Lord Syrael's parasites blasted through the layer of divine light protecting me and reminded me that he owns me, owns all three of us. Once the divine blinders were removed, I remembered the torture Lord Syrael and his fuckwads had made me endure during his ongoing parade of sex parties when I was a child. Grimacing, I push away the reminder of how powerless I truly am.

Hammering on the door brings me back to the present. My brothers are doing their best to break through to me, but Lord Syrael's parasites deflect all attempts. I turn my attention back to my prime directive—breaking Aleah. Raw sexual hunger sears through me as I survey my handiwork. I've manacled her wrists, attached them to a thick chain hanging from the ceiling and stripped her naked. After securing her ankles in manacles bolted into the floor and gagging her, I step back. Gods, I'd forgotten just how beautiful this woman is with her flawless brown skin just begging to be marked by my whips.

"Cass, let us in, you motherfucker." Tristan's fury echoes through our triplet bond, leaving me in no doubt what he'll do to me if he gets his hands on me.

"If you touch her, you'll cross a line there's no turning back from." Atroyel's anger and determination join Tristan's, telegraphing their intentions loud and clear. I shut them down and turn to my prize. Time enough to deal with my brothers once I've revealed Aleah's true nature.

I'd made good use of the time while Tristan, Atroyel and Aleah were distracted by their fucking divine mating bond. Finding a place where I would help Aleah see the error of her ways had been my priority, and I'd decided the protected playroom in Blackstone Manor was the safest place. By changing the locking spell from *'saor an spiorad'* to *'cuir stad air gach solas diadhaidh'* — stop all divine light, I'd ensured the privacy I needed to conduct the punishment session Lord Syrael had ordered. Next, I purged the room of divine light until all that remained was the cocoon of dark energy Aleah had captured.

I found a jar of healing ointment and used it to reduce the heat searing through each of the wounds the sex demon lord's whip had cut into my body, but only time would heal the scars in my soul. Nothing got rid of the awful buzzing sensation taking place in every cell of my body telling me to stop. Blocking the hideous sensation and the intrusive feeling that what I'm about to do isn't right, I carefully select my first implements of punishment. A double-sided paddle will do nicely to warm her ass and prepare the skin for the pain she's about to endure.

Not that I care, I tell myself.

I'll use a rubber flogger before graduating to my favorite way to inflict punishment: a three-foot Indiana Jones-style bullwhip.

Standing in front of Aleah with the paddle in hand, I use my enhanced hearing to listen to her heartbeat. It's a sonic sense that allows me to hear a heartbeat from thirty feet away but standing up close and personal intimidates…or at least it's meant to, although it doesn't seem to work with Aleah. Her heart rate is a touch faster than usual, yet I detect no fear, only resignation. The message radiating from her dark eyes couldn't make me feel more miserable if I tried.

"Go ahead, Cass. Do what you need to do. I forgive you."

Or maybe it's my guilt talking, guilt that's squeezing past Lord Syrael's dark magic.

"I'm here to prepare you for your meeting with Lord Syrael. Will you submit to him? Say yes, and I will go easier on you."

Those brown eyes watch me steadily, and she shakes her head, resolve firm. Without further ado, I move to her side and deliver fifty strokes with the paddle to each buttock in rapid succession. Pain releases adrenaline, which in turn increases her heart rate, but she takes the beating without making a sound, something that drives me to hit her even harder.

I make a show of trading the paddle for the flogger before retaking my position before her. Tears brim her eyes, but none fall, and she continues to regard me steadily.

"You can stop this, Aleah. Agree to submit to Lord Syrael, and all this will stop." I try to channel some care and empathy through the cold blackness taking hold of my system.

Again, Aleah shakes her head, resolve steady. *"It will take a lot more than pain to break me, Cass."* I swear I hear the words ringing through my head as I take a flogging stance.

The heavy strands of the rubber flogger deliver a sharp, intense sting that's sure to break through her determination. I take my time laying a crisscross pattern over her ass and thighs and relish in watching the impacts turn the red discoloration to purple. This time when I check, she's breathing rapidly while tears and snot stream down her face, but she's no less defiant.

I take up the bullwhip before grabbing her chin. "Why are you making me do this?" I ask. "Why do you insist on forcing me to hurt you?"

For a split second, I see shame trigger in her eyes and rejoice in the corresponding jolt of triumph that bolts through me. But her fucking indomitable will power is more potent than any shame. She straightens her shoulders and raises her head as her white-blue grace forms a mist around her.

Aleah sniffles and clears her throat. "We all make choices, Cass." Her voice is broken yet strong, showing it will take more than a severe flogging to break this woman.

Time for edge play. Lord Syrael's voice booms through my psyche as if he's standing beside me and propels me to the tray of knives I'd sneaked in earlier. Breath and knife play are a deadly combination playing on people's deepest fear, the fear of death. Knowing Aleah's morbid fear of knives increases the psychological terror factor exponentially.

The buzzing in my cells multiplies as I pick up a large butcher knife and move back to Aleah. Fear and pain glaze her normally radiant brown eyes, but they widen with compassion and empathy that almost bring me to my knees. Her breathing and heartbeat quicken, but she doesn't flinch as I wrap my large left hand around the front of her neck and place the tip of the knife beside her carotid artery. Then, squeezing my fingers, I slowly cut off her air supply while pressing the knife in just deep enough to break the skin.

As Aleah struggles to find air and stay conscious, she mouths the words, "Divine light protect our Cassiel."

The buzzing turns into a high-pitched drone that sears each cell in my body. Bright light explodes with a loud crack behind me. Agony blazes through me as the pain moves from the sharp sting of the fire ant to the pure, intense, brilliant pain of the bullet ant. In less than sixty nanoseconds, I'm firewalking over a bed of hot flames and nails. Terror and pain are off the charts incapacitating me, and I can barely muster the magic to open a portal and step through; consequences be damned. I can only hope I've done enough good in the universe to make my death relatively quick and painless.

A deep sense of loss is the last thing I feel before the darkness of Lord Syrael's dungeon consumes me.

16

TRISTAN

My bastard of a brother must have changed the locking spell on the playroom door. It takes Troy's and my divine magic combined with Nye and Raphael's Druid magic to reverse Cass's locking spell. Aleah is semi-conscious when we finally open the playroom door. My precious Ali's nurturing arms strain against the chains holding her limp and slumped body. I rush forward and quickly undo her ankle chains before lifting her slight form, making it easier for Troy to release her wrists.

When she's free, Troy scoops her into his arms. Strands of fear and determination weave together as they pass through our triplet bond, making it impossible to determine which emotions belong to Troy and which ones are mine. But there's time enough for self-discovery later. Right now, our Ali needs us.

"I will ready your bed chamber." Raphael strides from the room, anticipating our needs as usual.

"I'll go to the temple and draw strength from the powerful Druid divine sources to increase our healing power." Nye's ghostly body flits from one side of the room to the other, clearly showing her agitation before settling in front of me. "Is your healing power strong enough to break through the dark magic infecting her wounds?"

"My healing power is the strongest when having sex, difficult to do while she's in this state," I say.

"Our diaries can help boost Tristan's powers, but not enough to blast through whatever dark magic Cass injected into her." Troy keeps his gaze fixed on Ali's still form. "Whatever the fuck we're doing, it had better be quick. In this state, Aleah's too weak to fight the infusion of dark magic.

"Let's get her to the temple," Nye says. "The healing spring has powerful curse removal and can combat the dark magic." She opens a portal, and we step through into a large cave with a wall that reflects the blue-green waters of a deep pool before us. "Once we submerge her in the waters, her physical wounds will start healing in a few seconds. Then we can work on purging the dark magic."

I open my mouth to ask questions, but Troy, not one to waste time, sinks into the pool until the water completely covers Ali. Seconds later, she groans and starts moving in his arms.

"There you are, beauty." Troy's voice is gentle and filled with love. There's no hint of the fury he's holding like a lifeline. "You okay?"

I need you both. Now. Dark magic twists through Ali's silent entreaty as it bleeds through our mating bond.

"I'll take that as my cue to leave." Nye's spectre floats through me sending a surge of power before she disappears, but we're barely aware she's gone. We need to heal Ali. Nothing else matters.

I strip off my clothes and wade into the water. Troy hands Ali's warm, slippery body to me before shedding his dripping wet clothes.

Ali wraps her body around me and glues her mouth to

mine, activating the power of our mating bond. Immediately, our grace joins the magic of the healing stream to fight the darkness coursing through her system. Agony bursts through our bond as the two forces clash. Despite the pain, my cock goes rock hard with desire for our courageous mate. I deepen the kiss, speaking our love as Troy blankets her body from behind, sheltering her between us. The instant our bodies connect, divine light streams into the moist air and forms a protective circle around us.

Power and energy flow between us as the battle between our divine light and the dark magic intensifies. We each groan as our light kills dark matter, sending shards of burning pain needling through our bond, but we remain steadfast until none of Lord Syrael's evil energy remains. Troy takes a step back, shuddering from the effort of withstanding the force of such power. Ali twists around and pulls his mouth to hers, letting her psychic healing power flood through our bond until Troy's body relaxes.

She breaks the kiss and tips her head back, one arm around my neck and the other around his. "Better?" She's breathless but alert despite the energy drain caused as she heals the residual taint left by the black magic.

Troy nods, then gives her a quick, hard kiss before stepping out of the pool and gathering his clothes. Although she doesn't loosen her hold on me, her entire focus is on Troy. Her concern leaks through our connection as she uses her psychic energy to probe his responses.

"Are you sure you're okay, babe?" she asks. "Where are you going?"

He crouches beside the pool so that he's at eye level with us. "I'm not okay, but it's not anything you can help with. It's best if you stay here with Tristan to make sure we've removed all traces of the dark magic and recharge your system. I'm going to talk to Raphael and Nye to see if we can figure out where Cass is." Troy stands, opens a portal, and disappears through it, leaving us wrapped up in the warm moisture of the healing waters.

"He's decided to kill Cass, and we've got to stop him." Ali's brow wrinkles with worry, but the cave makes it difficult for her concern to stick.

After I take a quick read of her through our bond, I decide now is not the time to tell her that I plan on joining Troy in killing Cass. Letting her know that I plan on making Cass endure each pain he inflicted on her magnified a thousand times will take the edge off the healing love she needs right now.

She must catch a trace of my vengeful feelings before I seal them shut, but after a moment of intense scrutiny, she tucks a few strands of loose hair behind my ear and gives me a shy smile. Before she can speak, I thrust my hard cock into her. Her heat latches on as she welcomes the gift of my healing grace while we share our intense new love through locked eyes.

Our thoughts shot back and forth, showing our desperation.

I love you. Ali...my beautiful, precious Ali.

I worship, cherish, and adore you.

I'm scared.

Don't ever leave me. My heart cannot hide my biggest fear.

Give me your pain.

Never let anything come between us. We both finish with the same thought.

We move effortlessly through the water without conscious thought until my back hits a large smooth stone edge. The stone seat raises me partially out of the water and gives me the traction I need to shift Ali onto my lap. I tighten my grip on her ass as she braces her hands and feet on either side of me. With a firm grasp on each fleshy butt cheek, I glide her up and down on my throbbing cock, doing my best to draw out this moment for eternity. As she arches over me, hot lips brush mine.

"Gods, how I love your lips." I breathe the words into her mouth. "So soft, so succulent, so supple."

Ali moans as she breathes in the words. "I love yours more."

"I love yours most."

"There is no more than most." Ali speaks the words of love she's only ever shared with Troy before this moment.

Recognition hits our eyes at the same instant. We've gone through the ring of fire. Now, like Troy, I'm part of her DNA, her very soul, and joined, we have a life force only the highest power can destroy.

We speak no more as sensation takes over. Loosening my grip on her ass, I relinquish control. Ali grips my shoulders while she massages my cock with her warm cunt. I almost break with the effort to hold back my orgasm, and my breath comes out harsh and demanding. A split second before ignition, Ali slides off my lap, kneels between my legs and glides her tongue up the underside of my cock to the tip. Blue-white light laps over my legs and the parts of her body submerged in the pool as our grace mingles and swirls in its magic waters.

"I love watching you suck my cock." I speak the words, unsure if I make a sound but knowing she hears me.

"Well, that's good cause I love sucking your cock. We're a match made in the stars." Her muffled words are an accelerant to my already strained libido.

I fist my hands in her hair and surge into her mouth, pumping with wild abandon. She digs her fingers into my upper thighs and opens to me, letting me fuck her throat until I explode into a thick stream of molten lava flowing down the mountain of our eternal love.

Typically, an orgasm this momentous would put me in a coma, but one look at her quivering heat turns my cock rock hard. Maybe it's the magic in this place or our bond, but I don't take the time to ponder it. Instead, reaching down, I lift her out of the water and exchange places with her. The perch lifts her ass high enough to expose her rich brown nether lips as she spreads wide for me. I drink in the gift before bending to take my pleasure.

17

ALEAH

Tristan's hot breath on my pussy ignites the simmering embers of desire that have become my existence. He makes a tiny sound as if he's found the ultimate source of joy as he uses long, slender fingers to part my engorged lips. The brilliant smile he gives me as he looks into my eyes makes me reach for him. But he gives a slight shake of his head before gluing his hot mouth to my clit. Sharp shards of lust shoot through me, and I thrust up to meet him. He stills me with a firm hand on each thigh. My turn. I have no choice but to relax and enjoy.

Tristan makes sucking my clit a three-course meal, taking his time to savor each taste. He alternates the magic of flicking his clever tongue with sweetly torturous pulls on my swollen clit, taking me to the brink of madness. Time and time again, he takes me to the edge until I'm about to burst.

"Please, Tristan." I get his answer almost as soon as I send the thought. He needs me to submit, to release to him.

I relax my muscles and force desire-heavy lids open so that he'll see the truth behind my words.

"Please, master, make me yours." I submit and open myself fully to his demanding mouth.

Instantly, Tristan pumps two fingers into my pussy, pressing on my G-spot with each pass. Each thrust pushes me to the edge until I lift off. Then, explosive contractions overtake as I combust in a frenzy of pleasure.

I fall limply against the smooth, warm stone of the pool ledge but Tristan isn't done yet. Pulling me into his arms, he sits me on his cock in one smooth thrust and glides into the middle of the warm water. Nothing exists except for me, Tristan, and the pleasure in our weightless bodies mirrored in the magical light reflecting on the grotto walls.

This time, the dance is slow and sensual. Tristan holds me in place with a firm grasp on my ass while our mouths nibble and graze, teasing out every ounce of our feeling for each other, feelings that words alone can't express. Once again, my blue-white grace mingles with his distinctive teal grace joining the divine light streaming from our mating bond, entwining around us and weaving a safety net to hold us as we break apart.

I'm not sure how long we stay entangled with each other, but the throbbing in my left shoulder makes reality slowly leak through our blanket of euphoria. It's hard to see in the dim reflecting light in the cave, but I could swear that I see the outline of a third 3D triangle hovering under my black rose tattoo. Except this brand looks raw and angry, as if flames are trying to consume it. The new symbol confirms what we already know—Cass is my mate. I have no idea when we connected, but there's no doubt that whatever happened between us triggered our mating bond.

Cass, where are you? When I open the link between the new triangle and my heart, fear, self-loathing, and terror gut punch me so hard that I almost vomit. As I start to collapse, Tristan scoops me in his arms.

"Look at me, Ali." The command in Tristan's voice leaves me no choice but to look at him. "Now breathe with me. That's it."

His exhale releases a stream of teal grace that spreads a sense of calm through me as I inhale. "That's it. Easy does it." Tristan's words soothe me even more as the fist of nausea releases its ugly hold.

After a long, gentle kiss, Tristan fixes his frowning gaze on my brand. "When did that happen?" He doesn't mince words, and there's no mistaking his meaning as his surprise and shock flow through our mating bond. Cass and I don't have the kind of relationship to trigger the mating bond, so it must be the dark magic tainting our pure love.

But something had passed between Cass and me while he'd beaten me. Cass hadn't been able to shield his emotions from me. I'd seen the raw, savage pain and despair at the core of his heart. I'd connected with his willingness to sacrifice himself one final time to protect his brothers…and me.

"You can't kill him." I put force into the words to ensure they hit their mark.

"We can and we will," Tristan says with equal force. "It won't be easy, but Cass wouldn't have beat you if he was in his right mind. The dark magic has made him feral. There's no coming back from that."

He wraps me tighter in his arms to let me know his words aren't personal. He traces his hands over the faint lines remaining from Cass's wounds. His pain and resignation bleeds through our mating bond before he shuts them down and fixes his concern on me. As a master of ignoring my feelings by focusing on someone else's problems, I recognize the tactic. What the hell does one say when faced with an equal amount of determination. If he's anything like Troy, a frontal attack won't work. Distraction is required.

"Everything's happening so fast. The power in me feels

like a volcano about to erupt if I don't learn how to control it," I say.

"Does that worry you?" Tristan drops his anger like a hot stone, and he tunes in to our mating bond, igniting that prickling sensation that tells me he's using our mating bond to probe my emotional state.

I turn in his arms so that we're eye to eye. "What worries me is what will happen if you and Troy run off half-cocked and do something you'll regret for your unnaturally long lives." I beam every ounce of intensity I own through our mating bond, so there's no mistaking my message. "Something that will destroy our mating bond. At the very least, we need to hear Cass out."

A lock of hair slips over his face as he frowns back at me. I reach up and brush it back, resting my hand on his cheek until his expression smooths. "I just found you, Tris. I don't want to lose you. And I need your commitment to justice and truth to help me get through to Troy. He loses all sense of perspective when he sees me hurt and morphs into my knight in tarnished armor. He's mounted with his lance tilted."

Tristan barks out a humorless laugh as he detaches himself from me, steps out of the pool and starts pacing around the rocky ledge. "He's more than mounted. He's ready to make the kill thrust."

I silently watch the beauty of his muscular body, complete with that gorgeous semi-erect cock, while I formulate my strategy. Finally, when he's completed three loops around the pool, he crouches in front of me.

He gives me his megawatt smile, but it doesn't fool me. This time I see the man beneath the blinding good looks who's calculating his next move.

"You need to understand the law of the sex angel," Tristan says. "Using our power to wield dark sexual power is punishable by death. Cassiel knows this better than anyone, as he's delivered more than one death sentence.

I lean into his glare until we're almost nose to nose. Temper to temper, only this time, I'm not intimidated. A solid wall of love supports the heat in piercing blue eyes that make it clear there's no going to our respective corners for this debate. For a split second, muscle memory makes the fear of reprisal bolt through me, but the chamber in my heart that belongs to Tristan is as rock-solid as his sense of fairness and justice. I smile at Tristan and snag Tristan's discarded shirt. It will be much easier for me to argue with a lover clothed. Tristan follows suit with his pants, and soon we're facing off.

"You need to understand the law of Aleah. Lord Syrael did horrible things to Cass—"

"No, he did not. I'd know if he did. I'd sense it through our triplet bond."

But I see that one second of hesitation and go in for the kill. I stab him with my pointer finger. "You did sense something, be honest." I stab him again. "You just didn't want to know, so you turned a blind eye." The second those words leave my mouth, I realize how they must sound. I open my palm and lay it on his chest.

"That sounds as if I blame you, and I don't. I'm not judging."

Tristan covers my palm and tips my chin with his other hand. "You can stop worrying, babe. You see me. I can feel it in here." Again, he gives the hand over his heart a squeeze and this time, his smile tells me that he loves me through eternity and beyond. "Much as I'd love for this to be our next argument so we can have hot make-up sex, this isn't it. You're right. Cass deserves to be heard before we sentence him. But we'll do it together or not at all."

Our stare-down quickly turns into a can't-keep-my-hands-off-you kiss that leaves us panting for air when our lips break apart, and the glare-down continues.

"I need your word that you won't try to talk to Cass on your own, Ali." Tristan's soft plea batters at my resistance, but his following words tear through them. "You take too many chances, *mon chou*, and I can't lose you."

18

ATROYEL

I cradle a drink and try not to be impatient as I wait for Aleah and Tristan. I'm fucked up over Cass attacking Aleah, and I need her kick-your-ass and love-you-to-bits combo to help me put things right in my head and heart.

When I saw Aleah's bound and bleeding body, something in me snapped, and I became fixated on one thing—killing Cass, the bastard who'd done this to her. It was my job to keep Aleah safe. I should have stopped him.

If I hadn't had my head up my ass, I'd have seen the signs. Something had been off with Cass from the moment we'd reunited. Yes, it had been easy to attribute his off behavior to years of separation. Too easy. But the moment I saw her beaten and bloody, her past torture suffered at the hands of her foster father became blindingly clear. It had taken years for me to coax the details of the years of beatings and rape she'd endured. How her calls for help had been ignored by the very adults who were sworn to keep her safe. Sadly, it was easier for the adults around her to turn a blind eye and remain silent than confront the wrong that had been done to her.

Aleah'd been beaten and abused as a child, but something in her refused to break. I'd been sent to find and protect her, and I'd kept her safe. But I'd never confronted the men who'd abused her, including her wretch of a foster father. Aleah had insisted it wasn't my place to take vengeance, and frankly, it had been easier not to.

Well, not this time. Because this time it happened on my watch, and I will not look away. I will not allow anyone to hurt her again. Dark magic has poisoned Cass, and there's only one thing that can be done with a feral animal—put him down. Aleah will have to understand that no matter how saintly we angels pretend to be, sex angel lords are avengers, and Cass crossed the abyss, so he has to be dealt with. It's what he'd want. I'll make it quick and painless.

So, killing Cass was precisely what I planned to do when I opened our triplet connection and located Cass right after we found Aleah. I'd taken a moment to enjoy the increase of my powers. Despite the twenty-year hiatus from using my angelic powers, I'm able to use the enhanced powers as if I've had them for a thousand years. There was so much power flowing through me, I suspected it was a temporary burst, but I had enough power to kill my brother. Normally, it takes two Sex Angel Lords to kill one of our own, but I'd decided to take action instead of diving into my usual introspective state.

So, I honed in on Cass's location and found him in a dungeon deep under the Pandemonium Club. I cloaked my appearance with an invisibility glamor using my enhanced powers before stepping through a portal into the dark space.

Ironically, Cass hung suspended from the ceiling like he'd bound Aleah, only his feet barely touched the floor. A web of dark light attacked the cocoon of blue-white divine light encircling his battered and broken body. His wings were unfurled, with one of them almost ripped from his body. Agony bled through our triplet bond.

Cass slowly raised his chin in my direction and brought his tortured gaze to rest on me as if he sensed my presence.

"Atroyel, leave now before they get back. If he finds you here, he'll kill you." Cass's throaty voice still held the edge of command even in his weakened state.

But this time, his voice triggered a memory of a scared teen, arms outspread, protecting Tristan and me from Lord Syrael when he'd come for us as boys. Now, I remembered all those times Cass had gone off to do Lord Syrael's "special" work that had been so super-secret, Lord Syrael had used a silencing spell to ensure Cass never told anyone.

With this revelation, all thought of killing Cass turned to rescuing him. "We've got to get you out of here. Fuck! Where's Tristan when we need him?" I deflected Cass's attention to Tristan while I desperately tried to undo the chains binding Cass, but even my enhanced power wasn't strong enough to combat Lord Syrael's binding spell.

The distraction had worked for a moment as Cass's despair turned to panic. "Isn't he with Aleah? You've got to find her before Syrael's henchmen get their hands on her."

"Calm down before you rupture something." I grimace at the harshness of my tone as I react to the pain bleeding through our bond. Although Cass has managed to keep this from us, whatever block shielding his secrets is gone. Right about now, I'd love for one of Syrael's henchmen to step in front of me. I could use a good punching bag.

Stay present, Troy. That calm assurance had flowed through our mating bond, stopping my panic with the current of Aleah's love and hope.

"Tristan's with Aleah, Cass we have to go now—"

"And this time, don't hold back. If Cassiel doesn't submit,

kill the bastard." Lord Syrael's voice echoed from the hall as hard footfalls approached.

"I'm getting exactly what I deserve and you know it. Death is the best outcome for all of us. She needs you. Take care of her for all of us. Now go. Get out of here, brother, leave me. Save yourself before they get back." Cass's despair and terror hit me with the force of a blow, driving me through the portal that opened behind me.

Raphael was waiting on the other side with a bottle of bourbon that I snatched. I marched straight to the library, not giving one damn how rude I was being and have been brooding over our situation while I waited for Aleah and Tristan to return.

And now they're back, and I'm no closer to a solution than I'd been hours ago. Although our mating bond warns me that we're in for a session of tense emotion, Aleah's ferocity hits hard. She and Tristan enter the library in the middle of an intense argument about Cass. They're either ignoring or oblivious to my presence in the dim light. I stared in stunned amazement as the two approach awash in glowing angelicgrace.

"You haven't convinced me, babe. Cass is going to feel every one of your wounds one-hundred times worse than what you suffered. I'm going to take that knife and strip his skin inch by inch." Tristan's righteous anger seeps into me and tries to take me to a dark place. "Before he dies," Tristan continues, "Cass will know once and for all that some things go beyond our triplet bond.

"Nobody's killing anybody, especially without a trial. Let's put the testosterone away for a goddamn minute and take a breath. Jesus, you make it hard for a woman to come from a place of empathy." With that pronouncement, my beauty walks over to the drink cart and pours herself a large tumbler of wine as she steels herself. I've had plenty of experience to know that she's using every second of this break to line up her arsenal before she starts to kick ass.

I walk out of the shadows and cross to Aleah. She drops the decanter of wine and the goblet on the tray, wraps her arms around my neck and lets her kiss show me how much she's missed me. "My love," she whispers in my ear before releasing me and grabbing her wineglass.

I allow myself a moment to drink in the love and empathy flowing through our bond. Gods how I love this woman. For the longest time, I'd been afraid of losing her love, of not deserving it. After all, why would she want an asshole like me? I spent my time hiding from the world while she faced it down with a level of ferocity and determination.

"Have a seat, boys." Aleah's calm tone doesn't fool me for a minute. She's got something on her mind, and it's usually something I'm not going to like.

Tristan looks over at me and quirks an eyebrow… *What are we in for?* For a moment, I almost feel sorry for my brother. More than once, I'd confronted Aleah with righteous indignation about some slight or other, only to have her take me out at the knees as she ruthlessly strips through the layers to reveal what an asshole I'm being. But, this time, it looks as if we're both in for it.

When we don't move, Aleah turns with the wineglass and points to two chairs in front of the desk. "Sit."

The ice in that one word makes it clear we've entered Aleah's don't-fuck-with-me zone. We sit. She strides over, sets the glass down, and pulls herself onto the desk facing us. Not exactly a power position but one that demonstrates that she means business. The softening of her expression doesn't fool me. I've seen every tiny piece of good, bad, and ugly my beauty thinks she possesses, so I know only too well her passive expression hides some rather ruthless assessment and calculation. And I love and cherish every moment with her, even as I prepare to endure her wrath.

"Just so we're clear, Cass is your brother, and we now know beyond a shadow of a doubt that the universe chose all of you to be my mates. That means you'll kill Cass over my dead body, which, in turn, means you'll die. Because if one of us dies, we all die. That much I know from the angel of death. So, let's move beyond kill-Cass mode and figure out how we're going to rescue him." She starts right in without a preamble. No surprise there.

I open my mouth to retort and get her small hand in front of my face. "And to do that, you two need to forgive him." She gives me a grim grin. "Your turn."

But Tristan beats me to the punch as he leaps to his feet and starts pacing. "I am not going to forgive the son of a bitch. He went over to the dark side. That's unforgivable." My brother can be more rigid in his ideas when he thinks there's an injustice than me, and that's saying something.

"I can sense Cass's struggle. I can feel it in our bond." Aleah's face transforms as she bestows a smile on Tristan as if he's given her the best gift. "Let's talk about that, shall we? Why would Cass go to the dark side? From what I can see, that's not at all like him. He strikes me as the type who would go to any lengths to protect those he loves." She drops that little nugget into the pot and lets it melt our anger, stopping us short. Why, indeed?

"I need you both to listen to me," I say. "I saw Cass strung up in the basement of the sex club. Tortured." I meet my beloved's penetrating gaze. "He asked me to make sure you're protected and taken care of for all time. He forced me out of that basement through a portal to save my life. While I was with him, I had a flashback, a memory was triggered. Lord Syrael and his friends sexually abused Cass when we were young." I send the stream of images through our bond.

Tristan gasps, visibly shaken. Then he walks on wooden legs to the bar and helps himself to a glass of bourbon. I stay silent, trying to unsee the images that have changed my world view forever. Because deep down, very deep down inside, Tristan and I both always knew that something terrible happened to Cass when we were boys. The passing centuries may have made it easy to bury all memory of that terrible time, but now that the proverbial bandage that covered our eyes is ripped off, we can't help but see the gaping wound.

19

TRISTAN

I want so badly to crawl back under the big-brother-as-knight fantasy that has defined Cass for me as the images of Cass's childhood abuse stream through our triplet bond. In his weakened state, he can't maintain the spell blocking those experiences from Troy and me. I'd always wondered why Cass kept himself apart from us, and now I know. Cass was protecting us from Lord Syrael and ourselves.

As boys, Troy's emotion absorption powers had been so strong that almost any emotion caused him extreme pain. It was my job to help Troy learn to deal with his power and protect him while Cass had been off "taking care of business." But dealing with Troy's pain had been all I could handle, making it easy to ignore Cass's absences.

Shame washes over me at my lack of insight; after all, I'm the one with enhanced empathic gifts. I could have sensed Cass's pain if I'd tuned in. We should have been there for Cass.

When I can bear to look up, I meet Ali's compassionate but determined gaze. She's not going to give us a pass on this one.

"We've all made mistakes. It's what we learn from them that matters. So, can we put this talk of killing Cass to rest and figure out what we do from here?" she asks.

"No, we can't." Troy leans forward. "There's no known cure for a feral angel, especially one with superior power. Not even the gods have the power to fix Cass."

"But our Chosen does." Nye's sultry voice sounds as she pops up behind us. "Raphael, get your heinie in here."

On cue, the older man opens the carved library door and enters. "Madam?"

"Look. Do you see what I see?" Nye points her cigarette holder toward Ali. "Only angels with absolute power glow with grace. Hera forgot to mention that she's a Transcendent Nephilim," Nye whispers.

"That explains how she was able to capture the dark magic. The Chosen has come into her power." Raphael adds more flourish to his characteristic bow. "Domina, at your service."

"Oh, do stand up, Raphael. Would you two stop all the dramatics and tell us what the hell you're talking about?" Humor tinges Ali's voice, but the steel remains. "What the hell is a Transcendent Nephilim? Will this glowing grace help us rescue Cass?"

"A TN is a being born from a mortal and transcendent angel," Troy stands up and joins me in pacing around. "This is huge. Your glowing aura displays your divine status, and legend has it that transcendent Nephilim are responsible for keeping the afterlife planes in balance."

"You betcha. If you're TN, you can easily overpower most angels and demons, even in large numbers. You can probably take down Lord Syrael single-handedly, and with us at your side, you'll be unstoppable." I take a long pull on my bourbon then look at Troy. "So, what do we do now?"

"Don't look at me." Troy gaze falls on Ali. "You take it from here, babe."

I give my brother a nod, happy to see he's not threatened by discovering Ali may be more powerful than any of us. Status and position never did mean much to him. Ali needs him, and that's all that matters to him now. He's opened himself and ready to fall on the proverbial sword if needed. I'll do the same.

Ali sighs with the weight of the universe and, moving to one of the stuffed sofas, motions for us to join her. "I've spent my whole life waiting for the other shoe to drop, and it finally drops filled with a shitload of gifts—powers that I intend to make full use of. I haven't got it all figured out, but I do know that the four of us are even more interconnected. It's like you're feeding my power." She takes a long pull of her wine, sets the glass down, tucks her legs and leans forward, oozing intensity. "I keep getting flashes of things like Cass encased in glass and a battle with a powerful demon throwing fire. I get the sense I don't win. Are they memories?" she asks. She looks from one to the other of us before fastening those beautiful brown eyes on me, pleading for help and understanding...from me. My heart takes another skip of joy as she sees past the façade.

"I need you, Tris. I need your insight. I need your strength." The depth of her sincerity as it flows through our private channel almost knocks the breath out of me, but a thread of humor pulls the punch. *"And then I need your hot body. Not necessarily in that order."* But her attempt to alleviate my discomfort falls short under the burden she's shouldering and makes me love her even more. She will not bear this alone. Troy and I exchange looks. We need no words. Our Ali will not shoulder this burden alone.

"Let's do this, brother." I'm not sure if the thought originates with Troy or me, but that no longer matters. Finally, we're

united and have found our purpose—loving and taking care of Ali and each other.

I move to sit beside her, no longer able to bear the distance between us, and take her hand in mine, needing the connection that fully ignites our mate bond. Troy mimics my action sitting on her other side.

"They're not memories, *mon chou*. If they were, I'd be able to sense them." My memory manipulation powers allow me to access all memories, and I can't see what Ali sees now. Ali squeezes my hand as if to say thanks for trying.

"According to the ancient readings, Transcendent Nephilim can see the past, present, and future," Nye says. "You're seeing your future." She drifts around us, clearly agitated, but I can't tell if it's fear or excitement affecting her. And I don't care. Right now, being here for Ali is all I care about, that and helping alleviate the tension that's building in her. I squeeze her hand in reply. *"I'm here."*

"So, I can't shake the feeling that Cass and I are about to die. It feels like more than when I went into the Void." Ali's monotone doesn't deceive me. A cauldron of emotion boils beneath her calm exterior.

"Don't be a ninny," Nye says. "You don't die. Instead, the prophecy says you go into the Void until your princes figure out how to undo the spell Syrael casts on you." She sounds almost triumphant as she announces this to us.

"And Cass?" Troy's nonchalant tone doesn't fool me. He's no happier about letting Ali walk into danger than I am. All eyes turn to Ali. "Do you see anything?"

"Only us both lying in glass coffins side by side in what looks like a mausoleum or massive hall," Ali says.

"There, you see? Nobody dies." Nye taps the air with the jeweled cigarette holder she carries. "If you were dead, you'd ascend to Bardo. But you have to hope is your guys figure out which end is up sooner than later because you'll be in those glass coffins until they figure out how to break the spell." Despite being a ghost, Nye's skepticism comes through with megaphone loudness.

"Let's leave shame and blame out of this discussion," Ali says.

Nye frowns but subsides and floats a few feet away.

"We know from the ancient prophecy that Lord Syrael will make one more attempt on your life to complete the Rule of Three," Raphael says. "I'm not sure how Master Cassiel factors into the prophecy, but it is clear all three princes are part of—"

"The rule of three," we echo.

"So, what's the best strategy?" Ali's glowing grace comes off her in waves, making me wonder if stress increases production. She's equal parts glorious as she takes hold of her power and sweetly vulnerable in a way that makes me want to take her in my arms and never let go. And through our mate bond, I can see that she needs some of our loving care to renew her waning strength and help keep her doubt dragons at bay. But first, she needs to take care of business.

"We go to the Pandemonium Club tonight, we find Cass, and we get the hell out of there," Troy says. "And we stay together at all costs."

Ali straightens her spine and turns to face Troy. "That won't work."

"Why the hell not?" Troy retorts.

"Because the prophecy says the Chosen has to confront Lord Syrael and all this power oozing through me must be for something. I can't run from this, Troy." Ali uses hand gestures to emphasize her point. "How about this? The three of us will find Cass, and then you two will take him wherever you take angels for medical treatment? Wait, do angels need healing?"

"We don't heal so much as regenerate. If it's a mortal

wound, we'll need to take him to Bardo. If not, we'll bring him here as this is the nearest Druid healing center," I say. Ali nods but says nothing, so I continue. "We can't take him to a regular hospital for many reasons.

"Domina, respectfully." Raphael doesn't raise his voice, but it cuts through our discussion like a diamond through glass. "According to your vision, this discussion is academic. Lord Syrael will administer poison to you by whatever means necessary, and you will join Master Cassiel in the Void for an undetermined amount of time. Perhaps—"

I raise a hand to stop Raphael. "We've got this from here, Raphi. Ali needs to get some rest."

"What she needs is to learn how to use her power," Troy says, equally determined.

Ali gives a dramatic sigh. "You're both right. First, I'll practice using my power, and then I'll rest. Problem solved."

"Assuming you don't burn the place down with a divine light bolt in the meantime," Nye grumbles as we leave.

ALEAH

"Do it again," Troy points to the image of a mirror shimmering in the distance. "This time, make it disappear."

At Troy's insistence, we've been testing my magic for a few hours now, and I'm having my usual love-hate affair with his single-minded intensity. Once he starts something, he doesn't quit until he's done, which means being perfect. Or as close to perfect as he can get. As far as he's concerned, we'll be done when I destroy the mirror with both angel light and angel fire. Nye and Raphael had left long ago, probably bored out of their minds.

As usual, I embrace Troy's help—he keeps me anchored when I need to be. But we've long since pushed past my capacity, and exhaustion's starting to take hold. I'm harnessing power from something around me, but I'm losing energy faster than I can draw more in. Then, as if the drain from channeling my power into a weapon isn't enough, I have the bonus of needing to block the current of sexual passion flowing from Tristan so I can concentrate.

I do a mental ten count reminding myself I'd insisted on Troy's help knowing he'd popped into fanatic mode. I thrust a finger in his direction and give him my best bitch-goddess smile.

"One more, Troy, and then I'm done. We've worked past the point of efficiency. I need a break." I brace myself for the expected argument because I can tell from his level of agitation that he's nowhere near ready to quit yet.

Troy opens and closes those beautiful lips, gives a sharp nod, then surprises the shit out of me when he closes the distance and pulls me into his arms. "You're right, beauty. I'm getting ahead of myself. You did good. Tristan will take it from here." Dipping his head, he pulls me into a long, sweet kiss, only breaking it when we run out of breath. He pulls me against his chest, resting his chin on the top of my head. "You know I don't like this," he murmurs. "I just found you again. I'm not ready to lose you." His arms tighten even more as his panic flows through our mate bond.

I squeeze back because I have no words that can comfort either of us. The only thing we could hope for is that we all came out of it in the end. "How will I find you?"

"Yes, how do we break Syrael's spell?" Tristan comes up behind me and rests his hands on my shoulders, not intruding on Troy's space but letting me know he's here. "Any ideas?"

The tsunami of emotions flowing from my guys through our mate bond kicks me into caregiver mode. But now is not the time to fall apart. I've been in this place before. Time to pull up my britches and get the job done.

"Listen to you two." I give Troy one more squeeze, then step back so I can see them. Their struggle to hide their fear from me almost breaks my heart. "You're acting like I'm going to die or something. We know that's not true—"

"No, we're acting like you're going away, and we don't know how long for, how to find you or how to bring you back." Tristan's quickly proving to be the impatient one of the bunch. "Does your Nephilim power show you what might bring you back?"

"I keep hearing snippets of music and seeing a piece of chocolate-covered strawberry, and although I have no idea what it all means, I'm pretty sure you have to play my song to bring me back." I laugh at the look of confusion that crosses Troy's face.

"*What?*" The word streams through our mating bond.

"*Think about it. You'll remember.*" Then, a wave of nausea hits me. Strong arms pick me up, but all I can do is focus on breathing.

"I've got her." Tristan's voice comes from somewhere far away. Troy says something unintelligible as my vision blurs into the blackness of a migraine.

When I open my eyes, the dim light of dusk filters in through the sheers covering the windows. I'm lying in bed with my back against Tristan's chest, snuggled deep under the duvet. I move just the tiniest bit, trying not to wake him, but the second I stir, his arms tighten around me. He holds me tight, and his need to feel our love flows like a strong electrical current through our mating bond. The threads of my grace rise to meet his, and I let them weave the opening of our new love story. Time stops as our unconditional commitment to become all we can be blows away the storm clouds of uncertainty. Then, as calm settles over us, Tristan turns me in his arms.

"How are you holding up?" Divine light glows in his clear blue eyes as he probes our connection. "And don't even try to hide your feelings, *mon chou*, or I'll take you over my knee." His wink takes the heat from the threat, but there's no doubting the intent behind his words.

I run my hand over the muscle definition of his strong arms and the ridge over his retracted wings as I return his penetrating gaze. He needs to know that I'll share my pain with him, that I'll let him be my sounding board as I'll be his.

"I don't know." And that's the truth.

He says nothing aloud, but his message shouts through our mate bond. *"Share your burden with me."*

Troy is always there for me, ready to pick up the gauntlet when I fall but is happy to leave me to deal with things until I need help. But there have been times when I'd wished he could talk through a problem without needing to fix it and move on. That led to guilt for wanting Troy to be something other than who he is.

"Talk to me." Tristan smooths some curls behind my ear, and heat instantly coils between my legs. But right now, he needs my mind, not my body...And maybe that's what I need to but just don't know it.

I run my finger over the stubble on his cheek and love how he softens into my touch. "I'm not sure I know how I feel, Tris. I get like this before something big's about to happen. It's like when I'm about to have major surgery. There's always a risk that I won't wake up. I've gone flat on the table before. I woke up that time. Next time I might not."

He strokes my cheek in that intimate way that tells me he feels me and knows there's more but says nothing. I shut my eyes as I let the traitorous thoughts surface.

"It doesn't feel right talking about Troy when he's not here, but I sense through our bond that he wants me to work through my conflicted feelings with you. It's not that he's not strong, but when it comes to dealing with me in any pain, he's usually in worse shape than I am." The words rush out of me before I have time to censor them. "And sometimes, it would be nice not to have to be the strong one." This time, my words are barely a whisper as I reveal one of my biggest secrets.

"And sometimes having to carry the load makes you mad

as hell." Tristan makes the words a statement of fact I can't deny, but I'm not ready to admit. "And you can't talk to Troy about it because it hurts him to think he can't fix everything for you. But now you have me. I can help shoulder your burden."

He sees me. I cup his face in gratitude and kiss him, letting our bond speak the thoughts that have no words. Tristan gives me a smile that warms me from hair roots to tip toes when we come up for air.

"What I do know is that the universe brought me the gift of your love, and I'm going to do whatever it takes to bring you back to me sooner than later." Tristan pulls me into another long hug before taking my hand and leading me into the shower. "So, tell me more about this music."

"Ask Troy. He knows." I stick my tongue out before he pulls me against him, letting me know he's in charge…for now.

"He may know what will bring you back to him, but I need to find my way to bring you back. I refuse to lose you when I've just found you." He uses those expressive eyes together with hands and lips filled with love to find his answer. Silently and seductively, he explores my body but stills whenever I try to turn up the heat. It's one of the most intimate moments of my life, and unshed tears fill my eyes, knowing it will be the last for a very long time.

But Tristan's having none of my self-pity. *"Stop that. Show me the way."* Wave after wave of his love and longing hit me until I can't see anything but what we might share.

"So, if bringing you back has something to do with music, we need our own song." Tristan gifts me with a slow, sweet kiss, and I swear I can hear the opening bars of Atlantic Star's "Always."

On cue, he pulls back and sings the song's opening lines, declaring his love in a tenor as angelic as Troy's. Joy erupts across my face as I join him in the song that perfectly reflects our love. When he sings about us making a family, the image of the four of us laughing on a picnic blanket dances across the ceiling before dissolving and being replaced by the two of us dancing in time with our song. I make the same promise to him that I've only made to one man before. *I will love you always.* Our eyes are wet by the time we've finished singing the last lines.

"*Mon chou—*"

A blast of agony blasts through our mating bond, and Troy rushes into the room.

"We've got to get Cass. Now. He's dying."

21

TRISTAN

Troy blasts open a portal into a dark corridor, and his power sends a tingle of adrenaline rushing through my body. *When had Troy grown so powerful?* He steps through the opening, disregarding the cardinal rule against exposing magic to mortals. Grabbing Ali's hand, I follow him through as a fresh wave of pain hits us through our triplet bond.

Ali pulls her hand loose and points down the dark hall. "He's that way. So be quick. There's no time to lose."

Troy and I bolt down the hall. Ali's quick stride behind me assures me she's with us. Troy jiggles the metal ring on the dungeon door. Locked. He steps back and shatters the lock with a stream of divine light. The heavy door slams against the wall from the force of his power, revealing Cass's broken and bleeding body manacled to the wall with wings extended. He's unconscious, and his left wing is only attached by a tendon or two.

Troy crouches beside him and examines the torn wing. 'We'll need something to bind this so we can move him."

"I'll find something. Be right back." Ali's quick footsteps retreat down the hall. I use my power to release the restraints and help Troy lower Cass to the floor. Cass moans in pain as we move him, and his eyes flutter open.

"It's okay. I gave him my life for hers." He struggles to get the words out before falling into the Void, but he'd said the one thing that could blast away any remaining feelings of resentment we might harbor against him.

Troy presses the torn wing to Cass's back, trying to stem the flow of blood. He looks toward the door frantically. "Where is she? What's taking so long?"

It's only been a few minutes, but now isn't the time to point that out.

There's no sign of distress coming through our mate bond, but I briefly clasp Troy's shoulder in reassurance. "I'll go find her."

I cautiously stick my head out the door and check the hall before stepping into it. Sensing Ali through our mate bond, I follow the current of our mating connection. I've taken three steps when it winks out…just like that. One nanosecond, it's there and the next, I have to struggle to find even a hairlike thread.

I put on a burst of speed, round the next corner and skid to a stop beside Ali's body slumped on the floor. Her head's turned in my direction, and my eyes go to the bitten chocolate-covered strawberry resting at the edge of her fingertips. I crouch beside her and reach for her tiny hand. One touch and I know instantly that she's no longer in this realm or the next…she's slipped into the Void. Despite what the prophecy says, the Void puts her beyond our reach.

"No!" I bellow in rage as I gather her limp form into my arms. Loud voices announce company coming as I dash back into the dungeon cell and thank the gods that Troy already has a portal open. I follow him through it and only breathe a sigh of relief when it snaps shut behind me.

We step into an ornate crypt with two marble slabs sitting

on a large dais in the middle of the enormous room. I blink as my eyes adjust to the dim light and find myself staring directly into Queen Hera's stern countenance. Nye's specter hovers around her holding a large leather-bound book. A glance takes in mausoleum walls and floors made of white marble, rich mahogany, and gleaming onyx. Granite and bronze add accents to the massive space, and a square doorway punctures an external wall of granite, revealing a beautiful serenity garden. A rectangular skylight brings a single shaft of daylight onto the two slabs.

Queen Hera points to the slabs. "Place them on the altars." She leans over Cass's body and puts a hand over his torn wing. Once the wing knits back in place, the queen steps back and looks at us. "We'll give you time with them before we seal them in." Only then do I see two glass covers sitting on the ground beside the altars.

"We are not sealing them in." Troy's fury-filled voice grabs my attention. I've got to stop him before he his temper makes him lose his mind.

"Get a grip before she banishes you again. I need your help, Troy." I bellow the message through our triplet bond while the queen raises her lotus-tipped wand and points it at Troy. He instantly goes as still as a statue. With another flick of her wand, Cass's body floats out of Troy's arms and lands on the farthest altar. Next, she gives me a straightforward look making it clear I'd better haul ass and lie Ali down unless I want to end up paralyzed as well. I comply, arranging my beauty as carefully as possible on the cold marble. Her cheek is as cold as the marble when I cup it in the faint hope that my touch can somehow bring this beautiful woman back to me.

"That's better," Queen Hera says. She points to a padded bench between the two altars. "Sit." She gives another wave of her wand, and Troy's body moves with Hera's will until he's seated on the bench beside me.

"Their bodies need to be preserved until their souls are ready to come back to them, so we'll seal them in glass. Think of it as a preservation chamber. Don't worry. We'll give you some time alone with them. Now, let's see if we can work out what went wrong." The queen looks up at Nye. "Remind us what the prophecy says, Anais."

Nye flicks her cigarette holder, and the giant volume she's holding floats out of her hands, pages riffling as it opens. Nye runs her holder down a page then stops. "Chief Justice Tate gave the princes the power to shield Black Rose but advised that only the exchange of ether in true love could break the spell binding Black Rose to Earth. They must not try to convince or coerce Black Rose in any way, or she'd be lost to them forever."

Queen Hera heaves out a massive sigh making her disappointment more than apparent. "You had one job and one job only, to share your love with your fated mate, who happens to be the Chosen, destined for great things.

"That's right," Nye starts reading. "It is ordained that the Chosen shall lead an army of sex angel lords to eradicate all forms of sexual abuse from the megaverse."

"That can't happen if she's floating around the Void." Queen Hera looks at Nye. "Have we made any progress?"

"Yes, Atroyel and Tristan's mating bonds have matured to the point where Aleah can draw on their power. However, there's still work to be done with Cassiel," Nye says.

Queen Hera looks thoughtful. "Perhaps Tate and Bob can shed some light on what went wrong." She snaps her fingers and sends a message to summon the chief justice and angel of death before turning the spotlight back to Troy and me. "Am I given to understand that Cassiel has gone off track?"

"Yes." Nye nods. "Poor thing. He's never faced his demons, and now they've come home to roost."

"Your majesty, you rang?" A beautiful biracial woman wearing a black power suit and tailored white blouse walks into the crypt flanked by four paranormal beings, and all of them glow with divine grace. Chief Justice Tate and her four mates.

"Tate, there you are," Queen Hera says.

Tate moves to stand beside the queen, and her men line up in a semi-circle at her back. "Atroyel, it's been a minute and not one too soon, it seems. Please tell me you're not about to throw one of your hissy fits." She pauses, giving Troy a look that makes him squirm before turning a radiant smile on me. "So, what seems to be the problem?"

"The problem is that Aleah and Cass are injured, and we don't know if they're alive or dead, but I'm going to assume that whatever happened to them puts them beyond your reach." Troy's fear masked as fury is barely contained as he regains control over his faculties, but his gaze remains fixed on Ali's still form.

"What makes you think that?" Tate gives him the look women of substance reserve for men acting like assholes.

This time Troy looks up and points to the angel of death standing behind Tate. "Last time Ali went into the Void, Bob brought her back to us, so we know he has the power to do that, so—"

"Bob's inability to help means that only you three princes have the power to undo the spell binding her to the Void, although I suspect that won't happen until her work there is finished." She gives Troy that patient look teachers tend to bestow on slow learners. "Next problem?"

"Look, we've shared ether in true love, and yet once again, Aleah's been taken from me." Troy takes a condescending tone.

I rest a calming hand on his shoulder. *"We're almost there, brother. Don't fuck this up now. Ali's left us a trail of breadcrumbs to follow. We'll find her."*

Tate studies Troy then gestures for him to scoot over. She plants herself on the bench beside him and pats his hand. "Can you remember what I told you last time we met?"

Troy doesn't look at her, but his shoulders drop several inches. "We talked about our time in the forest when we met Aleah." Troy's voice softens with the warm memory. "You reminded me that we'd been inseparable, functioning as a unit, as a team. We have immeasurable power when we channel our magic together. You said if we combine our power, we can save her."

"So, what's changed?" Tate asks.

"Other than the obvious, you mean?" Troy points at Cass's body. "I apologize. It's hard to combine power when one of us is missing."

"That's because you're not seeing the whole picture." Tate pats the back of Troy's hand again. "We know the spell can only be undone by Black Rose's willing consent to be taken by her one true love."

"I've already done that," Troy retorts.

"Let's unpack what you're saying." Tate continues ignoring the interruption. "You believe that you're Aleah's one true love?"

"I do. Aleah may have a sexual thing with my brothers, but it's me she chose to be with," Troy says.

I stare at Troy, incredulous. *"You're kidding, right, bro?"* He doesn't believe that deep down, I can sense it in our triplet bond, but his panic seems to have driven away his ability for rational thought. *"Troy."* I try to reach him through our bond.

"Fuck off." Yes, the man's in one of his moods that only Aleah has the magic key to unlock. Gods, how I wished she was here with us. Meanwhile, Troy and Tate keep going at it.

"So, you missed the part about fated mates. You see, that's the thing, Atroyel. This is bigger than you. You two have the tools needed to bring her back." Tate stands and studies Troy again. "I'll give you a hint, Atroyel. Has Aleah ever asked you to do something just for her? Something you disagree with?"

"No." Troy stubbornly shakes his head. Our bond tells me he's genuinely baffled this time.

"Hmmm. I told you there was no easy way out of this. Wholehearted loving isn't easy." Tate turns to her entourage. "We need to check out what's been going on at this Pandemonium Club." She turns to the queen and Nye. "Ladies, always a pleasure."

"We're right behind you, dear," Nye says. "These boys need some time to themselves."

A thought starts niggling at the back of my mind when Troy mentions channeling our magic together and something I hadn't known I needed drops into place. Ali needs my mind and the way it works more than my body. I have a purpose. I look down at her beautiful still form. *I'm coming for you, mon chou.*

"Before you leave, can you get me Ali's cell phone? We need her playlists." I send a silent prayer to the heavens to give me a sign that I'm on the right track.

Tate beams at me as if I've won a gold medal. Nye's hand disappears into the voluminous folds of her skirt and surfaces holding Ali's iPhone. "Here you go, handsome."

Queen Hera rolls her eyes. "That's enough entertainment for one day." Then, with a snap of her fingers, they vanish.

"What the fuck do you need her phone for? Electronics don't work here, and sentimental crap won't bring her back. We need to focus on something that will work," Troy says.

I ignore my brother's natural skepticism. Ali's influence had made him better, but he still was a glass-half-empty kind of guy.

"Sorry, but not sorry, Troy. I see part of Ali that you don't, and sentimental crap is precisely what's going to bring her back, starting with making love to her with music," I announce. "We'll use the lyrics from love songs and your letter power bestowal to let her know how we feel." Something within me relaxes as I speak the words certain in the newfound knowledge that Ali needs me as a sounding board in a way Troy can never be.

Troy's face relaxes into a grin. "Ah, then my work here is done. Now, all we have to do is wait until Cass figures out why Aleah needs him."

It takes a beat for his words to sink in. "Ali's right. You can be a bastard sometimes. Have you been yanking my chain all along? Pretending that you think you're her only true love."

Troy grins. "Just doing my job. I think part of breaking the spell is us figuring out why Aleah needs us, why we're enough for her." He looks at me with that my-work-is-done smirk of his.

"So, what's the song that will bring her back?"

22

CASSIEL

I crack my eyes open to inky blackness surrounding me that can only mean one thing…I'm in the Void, although I have no idea why. I can barely feel a thread of Aleah's ether, but her last words to me echo in my head. "Divine light, protect our Cassiel." Despite my murderous intent, her last thought had been of protecting me, and I can't wrap my head around that.

And somehow, her divine ether had attacked my very soul. The pain was excruciating, and I'd been unable to withstand the torture, so I'd done the only thing I could. .I'd fled back to Lord Syrael and certain death.

Lord Syrael had unleashed his fury on me with his bullwhip. He'd beat me so badly that he'd almost severed my left wing before he left me to bleed out. I'd welcomed the darkness consuming me. I'd hoped to wake in Bardo where I'd prepare for my next life, or Elysium, the immortals' final resting place, but this can only be the Void.

I have a momentary sense of other beings before all-consuming nausea and intense pain force my eyes shut again. I huddle as uncontrollable shivering adds to my misery, hoping it's a sign that the angel of death will arrive shortly.

The Void is where souls with unresolved issues float in ghostly mist for eternity unless something happens to resolve their dilemma. For some reason, Aleah's landed here twice, and both times, Bob rescued her. Something had triggered a fragile bond between Ali and me, which is no doubt why I'm here in the first place. I just need to deal with the pain until he comes for me and hauls me in front of the chief justice and Queen Hera. Each of those women did have the power to blast my ass into eternity, and I can only pray they make it quick.

I need to think about something else. *Aleah.* A vision of her beautiful smile blots the pain, except the throbbing in my left shoulder. Our mate bond.

I'd been in charge of taking care of Aleah's security, and I'd done a piss poor job of that. I'd fucked her against her will, but she'd forgiven me.

The poem Atroyel wrote for Aleah plays through my mind.

> ***My Love***
> *She was a lover whose mind never strayed far from*
> *the scene.*
> *All the power pieces concealed in me responded*
> *fivefold.*
> *Our open boldness of speaking out and then usually*
> *acting it out was astonishing.*
> *It got so that the mere touching of one another while*
> *walking past each other could set off a confla-*
> *gration.*
> *As apprehension faded to trust, a cool sweetness*
> *settled over us.*
> *Time, thank God, stood still.*

I understand the indescribable emotions he's trying to explain for the first time. Slowly and surely, using her indomitable will, Aleah's empowered him in ways he hadn't realized at the time. She'd taught him how to live, how to breathe past his pain and find the incredible sweetness of joy. Aleah had offered me the gift of her love, and I'd been too much a fool to see it, blinded by my self-pity and need for vengeance. And now, it's too late, but what I wouldn't give for one more chance. I only have myself to blame.

Atroyel had been the first one to see that letting her in would be his salvation. I let my memories take me back to our time in the forest. The moment we'd met, Aleah's flashing brown eyes had tried to pierce my armor, but I was too caught up in my despair. But she'd seen past the walls I'd erected, and I can almost feel her small hand tugging at mine as she tried again and again to befriend me. Skipping, laughing, singing, bringing joy I'd been too dense to embrace. And now it was too late.

I don't know how long I float in this vat of dark worthlessness before a sound pulls at me. I strain but hear nothing at first, then the faint sound of Phil Collins' "Against All Odds (Take a Look at Me Now)" music track breaks through. I start singing the lyrics as I cast a metaphorical glance at the heavens and pray for a second chance.

Snippets of Atroyel and Aleah's diary weave themselves around lines from second chance songs and play through my head.

It is a good reminder to let you know that I do not take you or our love for granted.

Every time I see you or hear you, I think of how very lucky I am to be yours.

You are my treasure.

You make the best in me.

You remain forever and always.

Gods, how I wish I could see Aleah one last time to apologize and let her know just how much she means to me. Let her know I love her.

As I acknowledge the love washing through me, a tiny thread of connection starts to glow within me. It's faint at first but grows stronger as intuition flashes through me. For the first time, I recognize that I've harbored envy bordering on pathological for what Atroyel and Aleah have together. The resentment and jealousy only magnified when she stole Tristan from me. Because that's what my warped mind accused her of doing. But at some point, while Lord Syrael and his goons beat on me, I'd seen the light. Literally. As if Aleah spoke directly to me, letting me know that it wasn't my fault that I'd been raped and abused. That she knew my pain and was willing to share it…if I'd let her.

And suddenly, I'm possessed with the urge to sing. So, I start singing "If Ever You're in My Arms Again" and blot out every thought except Aleah. I imagine how her lithe body would move in my arms if she were there, barely aware of the music growing louder.

"Keep singing, Cass. I'm almost there." The command sears through the pain and darkness, piercing my heart and strengthening the new sense of connection. So, I obey and put every ounce of emotion I have into singing "Just Once." I let her know that I wanted to trust in our love, and I'd be there for her. I tell her I need her and ask for a second chance through the lyrics. I'm drained by the time the last chords die away. *Just once...*

My left shoulder starts throbbing as the opening chords of "Baby, Come to Me" fill the space around me, followed by a throaty contralto voice belting out the first verse. I float stupefied as her voice fades away but something inside yanks at me...hard.

"You're going to have to meet me halfway here, Cass." Aleah's voice sounds around me, loud and clear, upping my hope factor exponentially. So, I let my deep baritone invite her to come to me by belting out the second verse with equal enthusiasm.

"There you are. Fuck, you guys are hard work." The glowing grace surrounding Aleah's spirit breaks through the deep darkness allowing me to see her form. Despite her words, her tone is filled with relief and love. My heart breaks with gratitude as I look up into her bright smile. Even though our bodies have no form, I'd swear I feel her lips brush across mine, making all my pain and misery disappear.

"Atroyel tells me you like it that way." For once, I follow my instincts and match her humor.

"Well, our Troy says lots of things. Being a shit disturber is one of his favorite hobbies."

"Does that bother you?"

"Not in the least. Oh, it used to in the early days until I realized Troy loves to take the opposing side in an argument. It's not a side he lets many people see, but it's a signature part of his personality." Aleah's acceptance and love make me shiver.

"He's a lucky man." I try and fail to keep the envy from leaking through my words.

She sticks out her tongue at me, and her noncorporeal form slides down to sit beside me. "Yes, he is. And so are you and Tristan. You just have to believe it."

"Can you get us out of here?" Suddenly, nothing else

matters but getting out of this fucking place and folding this woman in my arms.

The grace glowing around her visage shows the graceful movement of her arms. Moments later she sighs. "I sense I might be able to send you back, but it's not time yet. As for me, well, you three will set me free. Until then, we wait."

We sit in companionable silence for several beats while I figure out what to say next. But I lean away from the discomfort of exposing my vulnerability to satisfy my curiosity. "Accepting your enhanced powers seems to come so easy to you. Most mortals can't accept the existence of the paranormal. What's your secret?"

The warmth of her shy smile seeps into my heart, forcing me to recognize it for what it is — the connection through our mate bond. I'm her mate. I let my heart do a few somersaults.

"When you asked me that before, you made me think," she says. "At least it did once I moved past the shame it triggered. As you know, I have few memories before my teen years and what I do have aren't good. But one thing I do remember is a strong feeling that I was born to do something great."

"Every child I've met thinks that. We all need to feel special," I say.

"True, and that's what I tried to tell myself. But I couldn't shake my feelings or dreams about being under some spell that hid exceptional gifts. So, I'd create stories about being born with special powers that needed to be hidden from people because if they found out who I was, they'd dissect and destroy me." She stops long enough to take a breath and rushes on. "And I've spent a small fortune looking for the existence of psychic phenomena, so I couldn't deny its existence when Troy possessed my body."

Practical, pragmatic, and determined. There's so much to unpack here, but first, I need to clear the air.

"I need to apologize to you." My voice falters, but I force the words out. "I'm sorry for all the hurt I caused you with my jealousy."

"Jealousy?" Aleah's surprise floats through our bond. "What on earth do I have that you could want?" Abruptly, she straightens her spine and gives a sharp nod. "We can talk later. Right now, I need you to show me your love."

23

CASSIEL

Aleah's hand sweeps through the darkness of the Void, and the angelic grace making her visible to me swirls and assembles into a large screen above us. Our mirror images stare down at us from the screen. My heart cracks wide open as this woman does exactly what I need to free my broken soul.

Aleah's eyes shine with compassion as she gestures toward the screen. "Show me."

On-screen Aleah, clad in a black gown, sits cross-legged with arms wrapped around her knees exactly as her visage appears beside me. I'm in a perfectly tailored gray suit, healed as if none of the past hours had transpired. I stand and pull Aleah into my arms. She rises gracefully, letting me enfold her petite body with my arms.

But she shows me the way as her rich contralto sings the opening lines of "Tonight, I Celebrate My Love," stepping back so her smile can invite me to join her. So, I do. Accompanied by some celestial orchestra, we let each line of our shared love song wash away the darkness until all that remains is the light of our love. And throughout, our growing bond becomes a continuous current from that new chamber in my heart to hers.

I don't even know when our on-screen bodies start moving, but soon we're swept up in the most sensual dance of my life. The woman surrenders control to my lead as I move our characters through the slow dance of love.

"You're my angel." I whisper the words as we move in perfect concert. Then, without missing a beat, Aleah tips her head and gives me a penetrating stare.

"Good. I'm glad," Aleah whispers back before moving closer and tucking her head on my shoulder.

I inhale her subtle scent, a delicate mixture of floral and spice with an undertone of sweet musk. In response, she snuggles in even closer and extends her long neck, physically exposing her vulnerability, letting me know she's mine to take…or destroy. After what I've done to this woman, her trust and submission bring me to my knees. I want this moment in person but realize working through it on screen with Aleah is part of my penance.

I trace a slow line up the side of her face with my cheek, and she nuzzles against me, matching my every movement. When she pulls me tight against her and nips my neck, my on-screen persona goes rock hard.

"Gods, how I want you," I groan. I need to show her that there's more to me than the dark side. "Now."

She sends the image of squeezing my hand through our developing mate bond, but her eyes never leave the screen.

"Show me," she says again, and I return my attention to our movie.

She rubs her chin along the side of my face before pulling back a few inches so she can look into my eyes. My eyes shut involuntarily against the heat illuminated in her gaze. My heart stumbles as her lips brush mine in invitation. She slides her hands down the arms of my jacket, stopping at the buttons. My attention is glued on the screen as I wait to see what she'll do next. Will she see who *I* am, who I need to be because of where I've been?

"You will be the man I need you to be. The man you are without the baggage." She steps back and assumes the at-your-service submissive position as if on cue, eyes dropped.

"I give you my heart. I'm yours to command, master." Her use of the term master tells me she consents to a master-slave relationship. Two things happen almost simultaneously, and for the first time, I understand what pulled my brothers…and me…to Aleah. First, she shows us the way to unconditional love. And that love makes me realize I have no desire to own this woman, and my need to control her vanished with the gift of her love. It's a good fucking thing I'm not in my body because my cock would explode.

I pull her into my arms, and we stand, lips a hair apart, breathing in unison as our love ripples along the current of our mate bond. Then, when my heart and cock are about to burst with need, the screen disappears on the echo of my angel's long sigh. The glow of grace around her turns to me.

"We have to stop blaming ourselves and forgive ourselves, Cass."

Those words expose the well of self-loathing I've carried for so long, but this time, her divine light pierces through and loosens my tongue.

"I can't help but blame myself. I was weak. Instead of fighting them, I submitted. I was weak." Relief washes through me as I let go of the secret shame I've held onto for so long. Real men fight. Hell, even little Tommy fights.

"I didn't fight, and I've always bought into their narrative that I asked for their abuse, that I deserved it," Aleah whispers. "But not anymore. Predators don't choose us because we're weak, Cass. Our strength draws them to our flame, making them want to destroy it. When we fight back, it gives them an excuse to do just that. By not fighting back, we lived to fight another day, and you needed to do that for your brothers."

We sit in silence for a very long time as her words penetrate the thick walls of my shame and resentment. The abuse would have killed Atroyel, and although Tristan may have lived through it, he would have been broken beyond repair.

"I'm not the man you need."

"Accepting who you are strips away the crap so you can be your authentic self, and you were born to be a bossy pants." She grins at me then grows serious again. "We're warriors, you and me. The abuse we endured gives us a special kind of strength and makes us walk a path only fellow travelers understand. I need you to make sure I don't stray too far from the path leading to the light."

More silence as I grapple with how this woman's insight and love have given me a life I'd dreamed of but never thought I'd have.

"Now, there's just one more thing, mister," she says. "You need to set things right with your brothers." She opens a portal showing Atroyel and Tristan sitting between our reposed bodies on marble altars.

I turn in protest. "But—"

She pushes me through. "Troy will summon me when it's time. He knows how to break the spell."

24

ATROYEL

The murky current of the triplet bond with Cass clears as the portal snaps open. Grace billows through surrounding Cass's still form on the altar before sinking into his skin. His torn wing knits, and life slowly returns to his prone body. He slowly sits and looks at us.

"I'm sorry." Cass's fear, remorse, and hope flow through our triplet connection.

Tristan moves from our bench and throws his arms around our brother's slumped shoulders. "There's nothing to be sorry for, bro. From now on, we're putting the past behind us. The universe gave us a chance at love, and I'm not going to miss one more minute if I can help it."

I join my brothers wrapping an arm over Tristan's, and the three of us sit in the companionship I had refused to admit I craved. Bless Tristan and his generous heart, one that gives him an insight into Aleah I'll never have.

"Tris is right. There's no point in recriminations, or I'd have to take the lead. You at least have a good reason for your demons. Me, not so much." I give him a wan smile. "I had no idea, fool that I was, just how much this woman gave to me until we started the double diary. And now that I'm re-reading it, I'm learning so much more." I close my eyes picture her words burned onto the pages of my mind.

You make the best in me. You remain forever and always my best. You give me enough!

"She gave me a gift even more precious than her unconditional love. Aleah showed me I am enough in ways I'm just realizing. That's her magic power as far as I'm concerned. But to some extent, my love for her has always been influenced by *my* needs. Unfortunately, that selfishness blinded me, so I didn't see that she needed the same from me." I stop to push down the lump forming in my throat, and Lord Syrael's voice echoes through the millennium from my childhood. *"Real angels don't cry, you sissy."* His many taunts had damaged me badly enough, I can't even begin to know what Cass and Aleah went through. Gratitude hits me with a flash of insight—Cass will understand what drives Aleah in ways Tristan and I never can.

"I fucked things up with her in so many ways I didn't see, but I do now. I think the key to breaking the spell is to give her the love she needs to realize she's more than enough for me." I pause and look at each of my brothers in turn. "For us."

"So, how do we bring her home," Tristan asks impatiently. "She says you know how."

I can't help the smile that turns up the corners of my mouth. "Oh, I do know one thing. We all do. Aleah talked about it in the diary, her freedom song. It would be so much easier if I could read her words." I sigh.

"And that's why she needs me." Cass flashes me an uncharacteristic grin. "Someone who can think past the obvious." He opens a portal, steps through to the manor library, snags the diaries and deposits them on the bench beside me.

I open our third diary and quickly find what I'm looking for. "Here it is." I start to read her entry.

It's now 8:07, and I've finished listening to Obama's speech; some parts of it twice. Followed by the David Foster freedom song twice.

Digression: I do so wish you could share my joy in this song. Not only is it the symbol of independence for me, it's just a great song. Too bad it doesn't have much in the way of horns. But what a full orchestra sound with rich bass bottom, and oh how I do love his keyboard. Oh, that you could share this—sigh!

I'm back. I'm having such a day, another of those when I not only feel blessed but am high on the pure joy of where I am on this day.

Thoughts are just tumbling down. I am so relating to this day in history on the grand scale and on a small scale for me. And you are the most crucial part of it.

It's been a glorious day! I still marvel that I am here and loved by you after where I came from. Today, I believe it. Wow! Yes, I've have been blessed to have a few such moments before, but each feels more breathtaking than the last. I could dance!

You probably have no idea why I'm babbling so, but you have been walking in very different shoes, ~~Hot~~ Hubbell. ☺

First and foremost, it's been 19 years!! That you've loved me. That I've loved you. How rich is that?!

I do so love you. The best part is that with David Foster, I dance for you and only you. On that pier in Florida, I danced for you, for me and for independence and joy I never thought possible. I'm not American, but I've had a journey of my own as a woman of color. And you've been there, even when I fucked up.

I'm playing the song "Winter Games" over and over…

So, after your love, that's who I've grown to be as a person. I won't babble on about that. Another time when I'm obviously gushy like I am now, you can ask me if you're remotely interested. But thank God that over the last ten or so years, I've been given the gift of learning to love and accept who I am.

And, if at the moment you're experiencing a moment of eye-rolling, remember David Foster—☺ oops—I mean, remember you haven't walked in my wee shoes.

I continue reading, remembering the first time she'd opened up about what it was like to be biracial in Canada. About why the Obamas were such an essential symbol for her. She always brought it back to that damned song, but I'd been too obtuse to listen.

I finish reading the entry and put the book down.

"And did you ask her about how she's grown?" Tristan interrupts with the question that shows another of my errors.

"No, because I was an ass who thought she'd said all I needed to hear about that in the diary. An opportunity missed," I say.

"Sounds like you missed quite a few," Cass says dryly, but love and acceptance flow through our bond, blowing away any hint of shame in his words. The joy coursing through me brings out so many new feelings.

"That I did, and now you two are here to help me make it

all better," I say. "But I can't help feeling there's one more thing we need to do before we play the song for her."

"Like what?" Cass asks.

"We need a song that symbolizes our feelings for her. Troy hit the nail with Zeus's hammer. We need to show Ali that she and all that she is, is more than enough for us." Tristan gets up and starts his characteristic pacing.

"We need a song that shows her you've learned to share her," Cass says.

"No matter how much I don't like it," I retort with a grin.

"You'll adapt. In time," Tristan says. "Now, what song will tell her just how much we love and need her, that she's more than enough?"

"You sound just like her," I say. "You two and your mushy sentiment were made for each other.

Tristan leans forward, forearms resting on his thighs. "So, work with me on this. Aleah loves dramatic, romantic moments, and she's had precious few of them in her life." He gives me a pointed look. "First, each of us needs to sing her a song that expresses our love for her right now." He looks pointedly at me. "And no taking the easy way out using a song you've used before." *One that was her idea.*

"You can stop looking at me, Tris. I'm finally all in with the mushy stuff. This is about her and what she needs, not me." I grin at him while my brain frantically tries to land on a song. Like a typical male, I'd considered romantic stuff a pink job, Aleah's department.

"Good. I'll go first." Tristan taps Aleah's phone and says, "play "On the Wings of Love." He closes his eyes as his rich tenor voice croons the love song. As the last strains die out, a clapping sound startles us.

Aleah's hazy visage floats above us behind a thick wall of something cloudy, but it's her. And there's only one word to describe the expression on her face—joy. I glance down at her still form lying on the slab before us, but there's no change.

Cass moves toward her image as if pulled by a magnet. "Play "Waiting for A Girl Like You." He sings the song as if every word is ripped from the depths of his soul. Aleah's loving face grows clearer but remains behind the barrier.

I serenade her with "If Ever You're in My Arms Again," giving each word every ounce of emotion I can muster. As I sing, the portal opening widens to reveal Aleah's beautiful smiling face, and she joins me on the final chorus.

"You're almost there, guys. I can feel it." Her voice comes through loud and clear, but she still stands on the other side of the thick plexiglass-like obstruction. "My turn. This is fun." She sings "Dreaming of You" as she moves her petite body in that seductive way she's never recognized she has.

"We're here, and it's night, so get your ass back here, beauty," I say.

She pushes on the barrier, shrugs, and gives me a grin that could compete with Tristan's megawattage. "I don't think you're done proclaiming your love yet." She's clearly enjoying this process a little too much.

"I've got it." Tristan delivers that shit-eater grin of his and snaps his fingers. He grabs Aleah's phone and swipes frantically at the screen. Moments later, Tristan points at me as the beginning chords of "I'll Make Love to You" start. Tristan unfolds his lanky body, moves beside us and starts singing the first verse. Cass and I join him for the chorus making the kind of harmony together we haven't had since childhood. For a moment, we get caught up in the moment, looking at each other, laughing, smiling, and feeling joy as Cass took the second verse. I get the break having the higher tenor voice. Aleah's clapping draw us back to her as we finish the final chorus.

"Okay, babe, bring me home." The edges of her eyes

crinkle with laughter and love, the most beautiful woman I've ever seen.

"Play "Winter Games," I say, and my heart sings at the rapture that spreads through our mate bond.

The portal blasts open, and Aleah dances through. Our woman shows us how our love has set her free to do the work the universe chose her to do, and for the first time, instead of being intimidated by her gifts, I embrace them.

When the song ends, she opens her arms, and all three of us walk into them. "Take me home, guys."

I stand, inhaling her scent in an eternity of bliss that ends abruptly seconds later when the strident voice of Queen Hera shatters the moment. "Not quite yet, Black Rose. We have a prophecy to fulfill."

25

ALEAH

There's only one word to describe how I feel as I dance through the portal, slide into my body and see my guys in the flesh—joy.

When the song ends, I open my arms and embrace all three. "Take me home, guys."

They continue to squeeze me in a three-way bear hug as if unwilling to let me go now that they have me back, but Queen Hera gives them no choice as she shatters the moment.

"Not quite yet, Black Rose. We have a prophecy to fulfill." Queen Hera gives me a stern look before snapping her fingers.

A burst of light later, and we're standing in a large office with a conference table sitting at one end surrounded by floor-to-ceiling bookcases. A gorgeous Black woman of indiscriminate age sits behind a large wooden desk at the opposite end of the room. She rises, bows her head toward the queen, then gestures for us to sit before taking the seat at the head of the table. Queen Hera sits at the other end.

Four men file into the room and stand silently behind the woman as we take our seats.

"Thank you all for coming." She looks at me. "Welcome to Bardo, Aleah. My name is Tate, and I'm the chief justice."

Before I can ask how the hell she knows my name, she gestures to the men standing behind her. "And these are my mates. On my right is Francis, then Bob, who some of you have met, followed by Nathan, with Caleb bringing up the rear."

All four are exceptionally good-looking, if somewhat odd. Even odder, Nathan swivels the purple guitar he has slung around his neck from back to front and starts strumming.

"Enough with the niceties. We have work to do," Queen Hera says.

Tate gives the queen a thoughtful and a short nod. "Queen Hera is correct. Now that you've broken the spell, I'm sure you want to hear about the next steps."

I open my mouth to release the torrent of questions that spring to mind, but Tate gives me the hand.

"I know you probably have a lot of questions. Some of them will be answered in the book of ancient writings you'll find in your quarters. The rest we'll tackle in the morning after you've had a good night's sleep." Tate looks at my guys, and a knowing smile flits across her face. "Once you've ignited your mating bond, we have a proposal for you. Guards."

At her command, two hunky men march us from the office through a corridor that ends in a hallway in an ancient castle while I contemplate whether I could call someone with green skin and wings men. Beautiful blue-and-black wings… and tails. Their wings are spread, spanning across the hall-way, and behind them, a weird light shimmers.

There's too much to take in, and it's all happening so fast, but it's more than clear we're not on Earth anymore. I'm starting to identify more than a bit with Dorothy in the Wizard of Oz. The creatures stop and open two massive double doors, folding their wings before standing at stiff attention.

"Your quarters. You have the run of the entire west wing," a guard says.

As the massive doors close behind us, Troy pulls me into his arms and gives me a sound kiss. "You okay, beauty?"

"I'm good, babe. Glad to be back with you guys." *And super eager to see you naked.*

"Ditto," Troy says. "But all that can wait. Right now, Tristan and I will do some research to see if we can figure out what comes next while you take are of unfinished business with Cass." He drops another kiss on my lips and heads toward one of the rooms opening off the great room. "Let's get 'er done."

Tristan gifts me with a deeper kiss before following Troy out of the room.

When the library door closes behind them, Cass pulls me into his arms. I tip my head and look up at him, desperate to make sure he knows all is forgiven, that we're moving on from that dark place. "There's only tonight."

He says nothing, simply takes my hands in his, holding them against my hips as his gaze rakes over me. He probes our growing connection seeking his penance for the hurt he's given me. I open my heart and show him that everything before this moment is now firmly a part of our shared past that we'll build on from here. Together. And I wait for him to take the remaining painful but necessary step before we can move onto wholehearted loving—forgive himself.

Eventually, that sad smile that's a fixture on his strong face takes on a ray of hope, filling me with more joy than I could imagine possible.

"Black Rose, my rose. That's who you are to me. Our

perfect symbol of mystery, danger, and rebirth. You've given me a chance at a new life, one I'd never dreamed possible."

Golden eyes filled with intensity consume me as he tries to find the words he feels compelled to speak. I open my mouth then snap it shut because once again, a voice within warns me to keep quiet and let him say what he needs to say.

"And it scares me to death." His voice drops to a harsh whisper.

I hold my breath, afraid that the soft sound of breathing will rupture this moment of raw vulnerability that he needs to heal himself.

"I've always needed to be in control, to be the strong one. I thought I deserved the abuse. I lost hope of ever having love or being part of a family, a community. All I had was my brothers, and they needed me to keep them safe."

I want to say something, to tell him I don't need this torrent of words, but he places a finger over my lips.

"Then you came along and showed us the light of love. Despite your youth, you were able to help my brothers in ways I never could, especially Atroyel, and I resented you for it." His head bows as the weight of his remorse almost crushes him. Every empathy nerve in me screams to take this burden from his shoulders. But only he can shed the shame that cripples him.

"So, I hurt you and tried to drive you away. But with that godsdamned determination of yours, you kept coming back for more. And now we're here, on the brink of something huge, and I wonder if I can be the man you need me to be. There are so many things I can't control with you, especially when it comes to you and my brothers. You're all so strong willed and take chances making it almost impossible to keep you safe." His head bows again as the monologue comes to an end.

I grip his hands firmly until he drags his eyes back to

meet mine. "Be the man you want to be, Cass. Be your authentic self, and you'll be more than the man I need."

We stand breathing each other in for several long beats before he expels a breath. "Okay."

He takes my hand and guides me to a sitting area. I have time to glance around while he sits and pours some wine. At the far end of the room sits an oddly shaped lounger sitting on a large rug before a brick fireplace. I drag my attention away from the leather piece back to Cass and point, happy to have something to distract me from the heat burning within me. "What is that?"

"That, my rose, is called a Tantra chair, a sex recliner." He passes me a wineglass before raising his. "There's only tonight." Shivers of love and anticipation run through me.

"I want to make my intentions very clear. My Black Rose and Troy's words paint the perfect picture." Cass flips open the diary and begins to read our "Exposing the Truth" fantasy. "Black! So dark that even night shadows ceased to exist as if banished to the depth of an endless abyss. She could have removed the mask. She was not bound or restrained in any way, simply blindfolded."

My breath catches as the words capture what I'm feeling about this man as if Troy foretold this moment.

"Strangely, she looked for the panic she usually felt when this vulnerable and found none. It was as if the mask allowed her to hide, as a child would shut their eyes—if I can't see them, they can't see me. Irrational, yes, but strangely comforting," Cass reads.

Cass fills my deep need for sexual dominance in a way that neither Troy nor Tristan can. Troy simply isn't capable of doing anything that might hurt me, making him hold back no matter how hard he tries. Likewise, while understanding the need, Tristan lacks the edge of danger and command that speaks to my shameful secret.

"Fantasy man wanted her to expose her true sexuality. Not the nice acceptable kind, but the dirty, uninhibited, animal instincts buried within her." Cass pauses and favors me with another of his penetrating gazes, letting me know that there will be no holding back with him…that if I go down this road with him, I'm committing to going all the way.

I'm getting so wet I can barely breathe as the words roll over me, each one peeling a layer of inhibition I hadn't known remained. I run my tongue over my dry lips. Cass graces me with another smile at my agitation.

He begins reading again. "Her hips pushed hard against the man's fingers wanting them buried deeper and deeper. But he just held them inside her while she desperately rubbed her clitoris, begging him to let her come. Instead, he said, 'No. I want to see more. I know you have more to give.'"

Cass pauses at this point, training his golden gaze of simmering heat on me. "And we both know there's one hell of a lot more that you've been suppressing, but no more. So tonight, we peel back the layers." He taps the diary. "Let's see what else Troy has to tell me."

"Her fantasy man began to touch her in ways that prolonged her torment," Cass continues reading, and I down a mouthful of wine to stop from fanning myself as each word takes my libido from speeding to racing as my body mimics the woman's reactions in the story. Although I'd thoroughly enjoyed this fantasy years ago with Troy, I react as if hearing the words for the first time. I ached for release. My soul demands I join with this man, my new mate. Yet, I want more of his heated tenderness with the undertone of danger and uncertainty of what's to come.

"He continued to fuck her until she came again and again, forcing her with slapping and penetration," Cass reads with a tone dark with a delicious threat that connects with my hidden inner place.

A moan seeps out of me when I hear those words and the trickle between my legs becomes a torrent. I want him to stop reading, rip my clothes off, and ravage me.

Cass lifts his gaze from the book, a satisfied smile playing over his lips before he prolongs the torture. *"Not yet."*

He continues reading. "When she thought he had taken her to a level of depravity she could never have imagined, he laid her on her back, pulled her legs apart and fucked her with his hard cock. She no longer recognized the woman who lay there, wishing he'd never stop."

Cass sets the diary aside and makes me the center of his world, rendering me speechless. "And now you're mine." He chose the perfect place to stop, and our mate bond tells me that I consume every conscious part of his mind. He instinctively knows I need this time to be about him, about us.

Although I haven't had much to drink, I'm almost tipsy. So many elements mix with my system's growing strength and power that I can no longer distinguish one from the other. But one thing is sure—if this man doesn't make love to me right now, I'll perish!

He uncovers a plate, and the hints of baked pastry, cheese, and apricot hit my heightened sense of smell. Picking up a piece, he guides it toward my mouth, and I get fixated on those long fingers and just what they'll be doing to me. "I believe they call these apricot brie bites." And oh yes, his deep voice does something to my lady bits.

Flustered, I reach for the food, but his frown stops me. "It's okay. I can feed myself."

Something shifts in the air, freezing me in place.

"Understand me, Aleah. I am in control when you are with me, and you will obey me. I have no desire to control you or change who you are, but I will make sure your needs are met, even those you ignore." There's an edge of danger in Cass's voice that tells me he's deadly serious and makes my nipples go rock hard.

"Tonight, you will do as I say or be punished. Are we clear? Now, let's proceed."

26

CASSIEL

"You are enough." With those words, my Black Rose had set me free, but I'm almost afraid to believe this moment can last, given our history. My heart hammers in my chest as I deal with all the emotions coursing through me. It's as if my toes hand off the edge of a cliff, and I can choose to fly into the arms of Aleah's love or dive to my doom. Aleah and the megaverse have given me a second chance, and I don't want to fuck things up.

So, my heart brims as a sweet smile spreads across Aleah's face when I command her. "Obey or be punished." The directive remains the same, but her reaction is so dramatically different from before it stuns me for a moment. Then, I almost go into cardiac arrest when she bows her head and takes the at-your-service stance. *Gods!*

I decide it's time to go with my instincts. I move to the Tantra chair and lean against one end. Aleah watches me looking every bit the sophisticated woman she is, but the growing current between us tells me she's more than a little timid.

"Come here." I keep my voice quiet yet full of command.

Slowly and hesitantly, she moves in front of me. I trace her bare arms with the tips of my fingers, and goosebumps immediately decorate her beautiful skin. Sexual electricity jolts through me, but love guides my movements. Lowering my head into her personal space, I reach under her chin and force her to look up, challenging her to react. She studies me from lowered lids but doesn't move as I edge down the zipper of her little black dress and let it fall to the floor. Suddenly, nothing else exists outside my need to give myself to her and to take her, *now*.

Heat emanates from her as my fingers outline the curve of her breasts. She shivers. I revel in the demonstration of her excitement, reminding me of the thing I crave. Thoughts that filled so many sleepless nights. Thoughts that I avoided admitting to myself—I want this woman, body, mind, and soul.

We stand in silence as I inhale her delicate scent and drink in her beauty. She's the most beautiful woman, and I take a moment to thank the universe for the love and acceptance shining from her eyes

I hook my index fingers in the band of her bikini briefs and draw them down her legs, waiting until she steps out of them and stands naked…and more than a bit self-conscious. She reaches out to unbutton my shirt, but I push her arms down to her sides, reminding her that I'm in control. Because tonight is about what she needs. She complies, allowing me to focus my attention on her breasts. I play with each, first teasing and twisting her nipples with my fingers, then my lips. I slide my hand between her legs and into her slick pool of desire. A strangled moan of pleasure escapes her as more moisture builds between her legs. I tease and torture her clit until her moans turn desperate and her legs grow weak.

"Lie down and spread your legs wide for me. Don't move. Don't speak."

Her lips part. I put a finger over them and point to the curved middle of the chair. Then, after a hair of hesitation, she plants her lovely ass in the curve of the chaise, lies back, and closes her eyes. Something vital changes in the current flowing between us as she surrenders to me, and I like it.

"Watch me." Again, my voice insists she obey.

She watches me undress, openly admiring my athletic body. My rock-hard cock springs to attention when it escapes from the prison of my pants.

Naked, I straddle her and push her arms up over her head. She closes her eyes.

"Look at me, Black Rose. I want you to watch me watching you."

Holding both her arms above her head with one hand, I reach down with the other, pull her nether lips apart, thrust my cock in straight to the hilt and ride her. I take my time, gliding my dick out inch by inch to the tip before burying it deep—again and again. With each stroke, I brush her clit against my pubis, fanning the flames of her passion.

Each time her eyes start to close, I remind her to watch me, to see me, to see who I am beneath the façade . . . and needing the reassurance of her love for me. Each command, like each thrust, drives her nearer to a frenzy so powerful that her blue-white grace billows around us. My cock glistens with her essence, and my left shoulder pulses in time with my hammering heart. Nothing else exists except my body moving in hers, igniting something I can't explain. For what seems like an eternity of agony and ecstasy, I fuck her. She lies spread wide open and captive to my will.

When Aleah moans and writhes, begging to come, I tighten my grip and continue my slow ride taking pleasure in teasing her to distraction. Finally, I increase the tempo, thrusting until our bodies convulse in explosive orgasms. Something in my chest breaks free as divine light explodes around us amidst a swirl of our mingling angelic grace. My joy is almost too much to bear as I collapse on top of her. "My love. My Black Rose." Wrapping my arms around her, I pull her close, not wanting our precious time together to end.

But we're not done yet. Tristan taps my shoulder, letting me know that he and Atroyel are with us. He gestures for me to move before changing places with me so that Aleah straddles him. She sinks onto his shaft, and he grips her hips, slowing the pace as his adoration bursts through our mate bond. The intensity of his emotion almost overwhelms but mounts higher as she twists to look at Troy as he spreads lube on his cock. He returns a look of reverence and devotion, then kneels behind her and grabs the soft cheeks of her ass, ramming his hard cock deep inside her. Knowing her inexperience, I tense. He's too fast, too brutal, but I relax as Aleah's reaction tells me otherwise. She gasps and arches back, moaning softly as she rocks between him and Tristan. I stand back and watch as their circle closes, grateful to be part at all.

Then, she turns, her eyes dark with love and desire on me, holding out her hand until I take it. For several long seconds, I'm frozen with joy as she brings me into their circle of light and love. Without breaking her rhythmic ride on their cocks, she pulls me close, then bends, and takes me deep in her mouth. I moan in ecstasy and go rock hard again as her wet warmth closes around me. I still for just a moment taking in the beauty of the circle of light I'm now part of. But our woman is impatient and knows what she wants. She grips my ass until I thrust into her mouth fast and hard. We slam into her as orgasms ricochet through her as her grace encircles us and pulls us to her. With some unspoken agreement, Troy, Tristan, and I lock eyes on her and push past the point of endurance, waiting for her final release.

"Come with me now!" When she screams for us to join her, orgasmic spasms jerk through me again and again. Our howls fill the air as our souls bind together, and we become one.

27

ALEAH

"Good morning, beauty. We need to talk." Yes, indeed, those are the first words out of Troy's mouth when my eyes crack open. Troy's lying on his back beside me on a massive bed, hands tucked behind his head… The perfect position for an early morning blow job.

"Good morning to you too, mister intensity." I stretch out all the lovely kinks and sore muscles.

"I can make those aches go away." Tristan drops a tray laden with food over my lap before leaning over and gifting me with a delicious morning kiss. As his grace touches me, the aches start to subside.

I playfully push him away. "Stop that. I like the reminder of our night."

"Is anyone listening to me?" Troy demands. "We need to talk." He reaches over and snags a piece of cheese from the tray.

"She needs to eat, then we can talk," Tristan says with matching enthusiasm. "She needs to take better care of herself."

That leads to back and forth. My men are so fixated on

deciding what I need that they barely notice me move the tray and scooch out of bed. I grace the heavens with a massive eye roll and head toward what I hope is the bathroom. Two doors later, I walk into a room that blurs the border between a garden and a bathroom. After taking a moment to admire the ornate bonsai growing directly out of the vanity countertop and check out the basket of creams and lotions, I catch a glimpse of my face in the mirror. The beautiful brown face looking back startles me. I push the curls off my forehead and try to figure out what's changed. My eyes sparkle, and my skin looks brighter...

Finally, I have a second chance at love—with my three guys. I do a little happy dance on the heated floor. I'm whole. There's no other way to describe it.

"Ali, get your ass out here." Tristan's voice breaks through my reverie.

With a happy sigh, I squirt some cleanser into my palm and reach for the faucet. No taps. Oh well... New and improved Aleah won't sweat the small stuff. Laughing at how silly I must look, I wave my hands around the sink area in a way that makes me think of voodoo before laughing. A warm tingling sensation sneaks up my spine mere seconds before a large warm hand clasps my neck. Cass stands with a towel wrapped around his waist, but that's not what grabs my attention. On his left biceps is the black rose, our mating brand. The newly formed triangle on my tattoo pulses in recognition. My mate.

"My Black Rose." His inner voice filled with gratitude whispers through our mate bond. He looks at his tattoo, and a joyful smile slowly crawls across his strong face as he slides his arms around my waist.

I look back at his reflection and smile, a little hesitant, not wanting to scare him off. "That, I am. Good morning." I turn to face him.

He studies me for a moment with those golden eyes before pulling me into a deep kiss that damned near curls my toes.

"Aleah, we haven't got all day." Troy. I'm about to respond, but Cass puts a finger on my lips. Mister impatience could wait for a moment. I trace my finger over the delicately inked petals, disturbing the grace still drifting into the air from our mating ceremony before leaning in and placing a gentle kiss on the tattoo. "My mate. My love." I smile up at Cass and use our mate bond to let him see I'm firmly shutting the door on our past and embracing our future. Several beats pass as we let the current between us speak what words couldn't say. Finally, Cass takes a deep breath and lets out a happy sigh.

"Take your time. I'll take care of my brothers." Cass spins me around, then reaches past me waving a hand once under the suspended mirror. Water spills from the mirror. He pauses, takes a look at his tattoo and grins at me.

"Cool. I could stay in here all day," I say.

Cass laughs, and the sound brings another squirt of joy through our bond. He's happy, for the first time, maybe ever.

"Not even I can hold Atroyel back for that long, my rose." He drops a kiss on the top of my head before leaving as quietly as he'd entered.

Deciding I'll take a long hot bath later, I quickly wash my face and throw on the thick terry bathrobe hanging on the back of the door. My ass barely hits the chair before my impatient Troy starts in. "Good. Now that things are all settled, we need to talk about how this is going to work."

"Can you give us a godsdamned minute to adore our new mate, Troy? For fuck's sake, what's the rush? We have eternity." That from Tristan as he leaps up and gets me a latte, delivered with a look that sears my clit. The man wants more than anything else to sink his dick in me right now. I gift him with a bright smile as I heap orange marmalade onto a croissant, but before I can say anything, Troy holds forth on all things Aleah as if I'm not in the room. It's so cute.

The next ten minutes or so play out like my personal rom-com movie, with each of my men jockeying for the alpha position. The intensity grows, but my mate bond assures me it's all good-natured fun between them. I'm a strong, independent woman, and they love me for it… But they're going to make filling my every need their new prime directive.

As if on cue, when I push my plate away and sit back with my latte, Cass surprises me with, "Tell us what our quad looks like for you?"

After a couple of gulping fish imitations, I realize that the three of them study me intently, waiting for an answer.

I lean forward and rest my arms on the table, signaling how seriously I'm treating his question. "I'm not sure what it looks like. But, for the first time in my life, just knowing your love is there is enough. We're enough. I don't need to plan each moment of my day righteously."

Tristan leans forward and covers my hand with his.

"I no longer need to ensure iron-fisted control over every aspect of my life to keep me safe." I smile again with the joy of speaking freely without fear of condemnation. "All I need is your love. We can figure the rest out as we go along."

Troy looks as if he's building up to popping an artery as he shakes his head, still mister intensity seeing every problem that might arise. My guy still has trouble letting go of his safety net. "That's not good enough. I know you, Aleah. You always need to have a cause, and the chief justice made it clear they have ideas for using your power. And we know that if you take it on, you'll rush headlong into it, danger be damned. So, we need to set some ground rules before that meeting."

"He has a point," Tristan says. "You do seem inclined to turn thought into action before the thought's finished taking form. We love that about you, but it does mean you take risks. Something you and Cass have in common." He zeroes in on one of my most vital strengths with unerring accuracy.

"Yeah, like he says," Troy says.

"Shut up and let her finish," Cass says.

I pat the top of Tristan's hand before taking Troy's, letting them know I accept the gift of their love and concern. "This is what our quad looks like to me. My whole life has been about walking into the unknown and hoping I had the resources to take care of myself." I look from one to the other. "Everyone told me that no one could love me the way I was, so I tried to remake myself while fighting to be my authentic self. Then Troy gave me his love and, in many ways, prepared me for this moment, or at least our relationship did."

I can't help but smile. "And one of the secrets to our success is Troy's constant need to know what I think, the main reason he proposed the double diary. We trusted each other and talked things out."

"And fucked a lot," Troy says.

"And fucked a lot," I agreed, "and for the first time, I'm not ashamed to say those words. At your insistence, I learned to love sex." I look into the heated gazes of Cass and Tristan. "And these two have shown us that we both have more to uncover." I glance back at Troy, taking pleasure in the ripples of his pride and desire riding on the current of our bond.

"Good," Cass says as he pushes back from the table. "Let's get this meeting out of the way so we can get back to talking and fucking. We'll take some time together. Where are we going, Black Rose?"

"Let's go back to the island. I'd love to spend more time in that playroom," I say.

"Been there, done that. We can find a playroom anywhere. I vote for someplace new," Troy says, suddenly the adventuresome type.

"I'm with Ali," Tristan says.

"Me three," Cass says.

"Now that's settled, let's get dressed and get this show on the road." Tristan jumps up with that sense of enthusiasm and gusto I love about him.

"Five minutes, beauty. There's no one you need to impress but us," Troy says.

After a few minutes of contemplating the massive wardrobe that happens to be in my size, I pick a black power suit to meet the chief justice. I have no idea what I'm in for, but whatever it is, I'll embrace this strange new world and all the exciting new gifts it brings... Especially the love of my guys.

I pour a drink of wine while I wait for the guys because, despite their protestations, all three of them do one hell of a lot more preening than I do. Not that I'm complaining, especially as I watch Troy's reflection in the window as he comes up beside me and takes my hand.

"Hey, you." As always, I'm filled with gratitude as I squeeze back.

"You good?" Troy asks, but he uses our mate connection to probe my well-being.

"I'm great." I open my heart so he can see that despite my worries and concerns about what our future might hold, with their love, I know I can do whatever I'm called to do.

"You've got this, beauty, and we've got you. It doesn't get any better than that." Troy takes my hand and leads me into the great room, joining Tristan and Cass. Tristan grabs my other hand, and Cass flanks my back, punctuating Troy's words as we walk into our future.

"You are more than enough, Black Rose."

EPILOGUE

TRISTAN

"We of the Tribunal are gathered to determine whether this mortal, Aleah Hunter, has the required attributes and values to assume the mantle of the Chosen." King Zeus drops his hammer on the stone floor, and I swear I see a collective eye roll coming from Tate and the female gods.

Thirteen thrones sit on a large dais before us, with Zeus sitting on the largest throne flanked by Queen Hera on his right and the chief justice, Tate, on his left. Nine gods take the remaining seats with the notable absence of Hades. Ali, Troy, and I are seated on the floor below with Cass standing behind Ali, protecting her back. Tate's mates sit on a platform off to the side. All gazes fix on the four of us.

Queen Hera raises her scepter. The king throws a massive frown her way that she ignores. Clearly, despite his title, it's the women who hold power in the afterlife, Bardo.

"First, Black Rose, the prophecy grants you three wishes once your princes break the spell. Your choices will determine our next steps," Queen Hera says.

"If she says, no pressure, I'm going to vomit," Ali's voice sings through our mate bond.

"

"No pressure and no need to vomit." The chief justice smiles down on her. "You have three wishes that will directly impact your life. What will they be?"

"World peace and an end to all hunger," my Ali says without hesitation.

King Zeus raises bushy eyebrows. "That's a lofty goal but has no impact on your life."

"I beg to differ." Ali faces the king of the gods without fear, and a burst of pride flows through our triplet bond. "Ending war and hunger will bring me great joy."

"How about choosing something a little more selfish?" Tate says.

Ali hesitates a beat, then straightens and looks over at Bob, the angel of death. "When I was in the Void, I saw ghosts floating around. So why are they in the Void instead of Bardo?"

"Those souls have unresolved issues stopping them from entering Bardo and the next step in their spiritual enlightenment. So instead, they hover in the Void for eternity unless they can take care of unfinished business," Bob says.

Ali looks down at hands clasped in her lap for several beats before looking up again. "How about ghosts on Earth?"

"Ah, you're talking about my friend, Anais," Queen Hera says. "As a Druid high priestess, her spirit remains bound to earth until she's able to pass into Bardo."

"Yes, I want to use one of my wishes to help Nye. She's been a huge help to me, like the mother I never had. I want to let her know how much that means to me." Ali sweeps her gaze over us. "To us. Can we ask her what she wants?"

"Why am I not surprised?" Troy mutters.

"What if you could have unlimited wealth instead?" Queen Hera asks.

"Wealth doesn't bring happiness, Your Majesty, and I make more than enough to pay my way. And the universe gave me my three wishes when they sent Troy back to me along with my guys. So, if I can't wish for world peace, I wish to help Nye then end sexual abuse," Ali says. "But first, we take care of Nye, and then we'll see how many wishes I have left."

King Zeus frowns again. The queen raises her scepter and opens a portal. Nye's ghost drifts into the room, looking from Queen Hera to us and back again. "Is everything all right?"

"Couldn't be better," Queen Hera says. "Our Chosen decided that she wants to help you. So, if you had one wish, what would it be?"

"You know what my wish is, Your Majesty," Nye says. "To be reunited with Edward, or at the very least to have the chance to say goodbye."

The queen looks at Bob. "Is Edward's soul beyond our reach?"

Bob steps forward. "Aleah and I can combine our power to reach him, but he has to agree."

Ali's face lights with determination the way it does when she decides to take on a cause. "He'll agree, right Nye?"

Nye bobs her head and crosses her fingers. Then, suddenly, there's a loud bang and a flash of hot red light. Sex Demon Lord Syrael and a large mirror stand between the Tribunal and us when the smoke clears.

"I see you started the party without me. This," Lord Syrael points to Ali, disgust dripping from his face, "human has what belongs to me. I am the rightful Chosen One."

The gods start talking amongst themselves. Shock radiates through our mate bond.

King Zeus smashes a thunderbolt into the floor. "Order."

Talking abruptly ceases.

The chief justice raises a hand. "Syrael, you make a very

serious charge. Do you have any evidence to substantiate your claim?"

"In other words, prove it," Queen Hera says.

Black and red grace stream from the entity standing before us. Lord Syrael turns to the mirror, and a large gaping eye appears in its center.

"Magic mirror in the hall,

Who in this land is the sexiest one of all?"

The mirror answers:

"You, Lord Syrael, are sexy, it's true,

But the Chosen is a thousand times sexier than you."

Lord Syrael curses and turns to face Ali, throwing up a fire ring between them. Bedlam breaks out around us as Ali stands and turns to face the demon lord's wrath. Blue-white grace streams from her body. Cass and Troy bolt forward, but with a graceful wave of her arms, Ali throws a forcefield separating her and Lord Syrael from the rest of the room.

"We've got to stop her." Cass dashes forward and tries to break through the wall of transparent light shimmering between us.

But Ali's attention is transfixed on Lord Syrael.

I'm hit with strong pulling on my power. I stagger back a step. *"What the fuck?"* I scream through our triplet bond.

"She's using our power to strengthen hers," Cass says. "Give it to her."

Linking minds, we open our hearts so Ali can access our power. *"It's all yours, beauty,"* Troy says through our mate connection.

Without hesitation, Ali pulls my gift from her jacket pocket and walks through the wall of fire until she's in front of the demon lord. "Dagger." The magical light dagger flares with divine light.

A flicker of fear and uncertainty crosses Lord Syrael's face. "Cunt."

"This is your last chance, Syrael." Ali ignores his attempt to shame her. "Repent your evil ways or suffer the consequences."

"I'd rather die," Lord Syrael spits out, unable to hide his terror.

"As you wish."

Power swirls through us in a vortex as Ali draws some from each of us as she walks into Lord Syrael's firestorm. Dark clashes with light as firebolts hit one after the other, but undeterred, she takes another step and grabs the back of Lord Syrael's neck. Then, in one swift movement, she plunges the knife into the dark lord's heart. Fire, divine grace, and dark ether fill the room in an explosion of fireworks. Bursts of energy battle, finally converge into a ball of white fire hovering above Ali's open palm. She turns to face the Tribunal.

"I've got him. Now, what do I do with him?" Ali asks.

"I think this is where I come in." Nye shocks the shit out of us as her material form walks forward.

"What the fuck?" The question bounces through our bond.

Queen Hera stands. "There's my old friend." Her stern face looks almost gentle as she looks from Nye to Ali. "You broke the spell Syrael put on Anais. Thank you for bringing her back to me." She turns her gaze back to Nye. "Time to work, Anais." Queen Hera holds out the ceramic jar that appears in her hands.

"I'll take him off your hands, lassie." Nye snags the jar from the queen, lifts the lid, and holds it out to Ali. "Put him in here. We'll perform a magic destruction ceremony at the temple."

After Ali drops the fireball into the jar, Nye puts the lid on, murmuring a power containment spell. When she's satisfied that Syrael's remains are secure, she puts the jar on the floor and opens her arms to Ali, eyes brimming with tears.

"You really are the cat's pajamas. You always have a home with me. You're the daughter we never had."

Joy floods through our mate bond as Ali walks into her embrace. "We can talk about all of that later. But, right now, we've got to get Edward back for you."

Nye gives Ali another squeeze before releasing her and swiping at her eyes. "We can figure all that out later. Right now, you've got business to take care of." Nye faces the Tribunal. "Majesties, I'll be off." She gives a low curtsy, picks up the jar and turns to the queen. "I'll see you soon. We have some unfinished business to take care of." The image of the two old girls doing the full-tilt group-sex boogie brings a bark of laughter from Zeus.

The stare-down between the gods and Ali pulls our attention back to the room. King Zeus opens his mouth to speak, but the queen gives him the hand. Then, standing, she walks down the few stairs until she's face-to-face with Ali. "My child, heed him no mind. Your altruistic and just actions prove beyond a doubt that you are the chosen Erogelic Lord. The chief justice will take it from here. Our work is done."

King Zeus hammers his thunderbolt on the floor. "This tribunal is adjourned."

I most definitely feel the stifled eye rolls of the women in the room before the gods bustle out of the room, leaving us with Tate and her mates. As they exit, four fae guards drag in six male and two female angels branded with Lord Syrael's eye and dump them in front of Tate. One of the men struggles to his feet, but the guard kicks them from under him.

The guards stand at attention between the men, with their vast wings folded flat against their backs. "Mongah at your service, your honor."

"At ease, Monty. What have you here?" Tate asks.

One of the guards bows his head. "We found Syrael's henchmen outside the great hall and arrested them. We were about to take them to the Sexy Sins Prison, but this one," Monty kicks at the leader, "demanded an audience claiming diplomatic immunity."

An ethereal light highlights the splotches of color in each of Tate's strange violet eyes as she surveys the group crouched before her. The energy in the room shifts as she studies them for several very long minutes. Finally, the air clears, and she stands.

"You are aware you're in Bardo, the afterlife realm where you're held accountable for your actions. Unfortunately for you, there is no such thing as diplomatic immunity here. So, what do you have to say to make me reconsider sending you to our darkest dungeon?" Power pulses from the chief justice as she addresses the man Monty kicked. "You may speak."

The angel remains on his knees but raises his head. The man's beauty rivals mine, but he doesn't attempt to cloak his ferocity. "We beg clemency, your honor, if I may call you that." He pauses and raises an eyebrow, respectful but making it clear that he isn't intimidated by her power. When Tate nods, he continues, "Demon Lord Syrael was originally a sex angel lord, who abused his enormous power." He points at my brothers and me. "Like the princes here, we were bound to him. He took us with him when the gods cast his ass from grace, stole our power, and put a spell on us, forcing us to obey." The guy throws Tate his best pleading-pathetic look, but she seems unfazed. On the other hand, Ali seems to be a puddle of empathy.

"Poor things. They deserve a second chance."

"They deserve death." Cass is back to his cut-and-dried self.

"Yet, these princes found a way to break free of Syrael. All we're asking for is the chance to do better." These words come from the man kneeling to the leader's right, equally good-looking, but this one oozes charm. "Doesn't everyone deserve a second chance?"

"Yes, oh yes, they do." Ali steps forward before we can react, holding her hand in the air. "I'm not sure of the protocol here, and I know you're probably got something in mind for me, but I'll take responsibility for these men if you give them a second chance."

"No fucking way." Cass.

"Beauty, this isn't a good idea." Troy.

"I support whatever decision you make." I, too, can be a charmer and ignore the looks from my brothers. We are a hair from celebrating eternity with our Ali, and I, for one, intend to start it off with a bang.

"Ha, funny." Ali.

"Suck up." Troy.

"Yeah, yeah. You just wish it was you." Me.

"Boys, we have plenty of time for this later." Finally, Ali's impatience breaks through.

Tate turns to consider Ali. "You know, that might not be a bad idea." She faces her mates, the high court examiners, still sitting quietly on the smaller dais. "What do you think?"

After a moment of telepathic communication, Bob straightens his relaxed posture and strolls into our group. "We recommend sending them through the assessment process. If they have not committed an unredeemable act, we agree that they be granted a second chance, but one chance only."

"Then, it's settled." Tate gives him a nod of thanks, and the guards hustle the angels out the door. Tate turns her violet gaze back to Ali when the doors close behind them. "Like you, after years of living life as a human, I learned I was a demi-god with fated mates, so I know better than most what's coming." Tate gives Ali an empathetic look. "And your first kill is never easy. So, here's what will happen. You'll take the next month with your mates figuring out how you want to handle this and come back to me with a proposal." Her smile transforms her stern face. "Nothing formal. Verbal is fine. Your priority is having some fun and getting to know your new mates. I remember those days. Now, we've got a hearing to attend to." Tate turns then hesitates.

"Any questions?"

"Don't you dare, Aleah. We've waited long enough." Cass's deep voice roars through our mate bond.

"I second that sentiment." Troy. *"We've got our own business to attend to."*

"Delay one more second, and I'll add warming your ass to the fantasy we have in mind for you tonight." My heart fills at the laughter that returns through our connection.

"Nothing that can't wait," Ali says. "Thank you for your consideration." Ali nudges us through the bond. "Guys."

In typical guy fashion, we echo her thanks without a faint clue what we're so thankful for. Then, with a parting smile from the chief justice, Tate and her mates take their leave.

Ali turns to us, grinning. "And that, gentlemen, is a wrap. We have eternity to figure out the rest."

Thank you so much for taking the time to read my Rogue Angels series. If you enjoyed this series, check out the Sexy Sins Afterlife Retreat, a paranormal reverse harem romance series featuring some familiar names ;).

Keep reading and feeding your fantasies,
Lilith

Join Lilith's Smutty Readers Email List and get a free copy of *Mick's Mission*, a paranormal reverse harem romance!

lilithdarville.com/newsletter

Chapter One
Tate

"Am I dead?"

Those are the first words out of my mouth after I land flat on my ass in a throne room. At least, I think it's a throne room. One minute, I was hovering above my comatose body, hoping the angel of death would actually look like Joe Black —yes I have a Brad Pitt fetish. The next, I was plucked out of the room and deposited here. Still dressed in my haute couture hospital gown, I might add. *sigh* Yeah, that's exactly how I want to be dressed when I make my appearance at the pearly gates. Wait—pain and nausea grip my middle. *So,* not *the pearly gates.* My head swims, and I keep it bowed while I take inventory.

I pinch my arm . . . *Ouch.* Okay, I have corporeal presence. Visions of the tornado in *The Wizard of Oz* drift through my mind. *Not the pearly gates. Not Kansas. Oz is also highly unlikely.* Then where the hell am I? I turn in a circle and find my bearings in the iridescent eyes of a stunning woman sitting on an ornate chair. Her flowing gown shimmers as she raises her arm. A second later, a blanket wraps around my shoulders. I tug it across my front, suddenly aware that I'm freezing. At least I'm not in hell . . . I doubt they have manners there.

"No child, you are not dead. You've been chosen for a special mission. We don't have much time before the transition sickness takes hold. Please listen carefully. My name is Hera, and I'm Queen of the Olympian gods."

"Where am I?" I don't care who she is, and this nausea is making me more than a little salty. If she thinks I'm going to sit here quietly and just take whatever she's dishing out, she's got another thought coming.

I open my mouth to speak . . . and can't. The mouth opens, but not a sound comes out. What the fuck? I glare up at Hera. She graces me with a guess-who's-in-charge smile.

"You are in Bardo."

I give her the stink eye. I studied the classics in university, and I know that, as queen of the gods, she has few redeeming qualities.

She looks down at me and smiles. "Don't believe everything you hear. I'm sure I have many good traits."

Name two.

"You'd do well to watch that mouth of yours. I've killed for less."

So, she reads minds. Great.

"Bardo is the realm between realms. Welcome. This will be quick because we have very little time before the ascension cold fever takes over. Right now, your earthly body lies in a coma, allowing you to do the work we need. You will take over as director at one of our schools for one of your Earth months."

Delight battles pain as I realize what she's saying. If this is the afterlife, I can find out what happened to my husband, Bob. Find out if our love was so pure that he's gone on to another life. My heart hammers with fear and hope. *Maybe, just maybe.* My teeth chatter so hard I'm scared they'll chip, but I manage to stammer out the words.

"Is my husband here?"

"Yes. He's here doing the work he needs to do."

My heart does a happy dance, dampened by this damned sickness that's overtaking me. "I need to see him."

"Child, I'm going to speak in your vernacular. Refuse to do this work for us, and we'll pop your ass right back in your body where you can wait another fifty years to see your beloved Bob. Or, do the work you're chosen for and spend the rest of eternity with him."

Well, that was clear.

At least I know how to run a college. But you can't solve organizational problems in a month. Definitely not. Nothing much gets done in the first ninety days if any manager worth her salt is doing the job properly.

"And if this examination center of yours isn't in order in a month?" I so want to give her the stink eye again, but she's just so damned intimidating. Everything about her screams, "Don't fuck with me." It's insane that Zeus was able to fuck around on her and live to tell the tale.

Hera showers me with a triumphant smile. "I have every confidence that with the examiners' help, you'll set things right at the Sexy Sins Retreat."

And speaking of all things weird, who on earth picked such a cheesy name? I mean, really. Of course, then again I'm talking about an entity that marries her brother who, in turn, cheats on her—

The pain ratchets up a notch.

"You'd do wise to park that attitude of yours up here."

More mind reading. Awesome.

"I don't need to read minds when looking at a face as expressive as yours. The name was my idea, and I certainly hope one of the lessons you'll learn is to be far less judgmental."

By now, the pain and nausea are so bad I can barely breathe. *I. Am. Not. Judgmental.*

"Ah, the ascension cold fever has set in. You'll need that taken care of. Once you're over the transition symptoms, the examiners will orient you to your role. Good luck, child." Hera stands and disappears in a flash of light. I lie huddled in a muddled mass of misery.

Wait. But . . . but all I can do is hold my head as a severe headache hits and intense cold racks my body. Then, I'm in the air and snuggled against a large, warm body. *Heat.*

I look up and catch a glimpse of brunette curls framing the most beautiful and familiar face. My mind searches for a thought it can't find—only pain and the need to get rid of it exists. Hera's voice, real or imagined, echoes in my brain.

"One last piece of advice, child, things here are not always what they appear to be. Follow your heart, and all will become clear."

End of Sample

To continue reading, be sure to pick up *Tate's Angel* at your favorite retailer.

ALSO BY LILITH DARVILLE

Wicked Angels Series

Dark Urban Fantasy Romance

Interconnected Standalones

Follow a team of fallen angels as they fight against human trafficking and navigate the blurred lines between good and evil. Set in Pandemonium, a notorious club where they blend in with humans, this heart-pounding series will leave you breathless. Don't miss out on this intense and spicy journey of redemption and second chances.

.

Rogue Angels Series

Dark Urban Fantasy Romance

Completed Series

Rogue Angels is a twist retelling of the Snow White fairytale. Enjoy an adventure with fated mates, midlife crisis, and evil demons. This story includes themes of love, sacrifice, and self-discovery.

.

Sexy Sins Afterlife Retreat Series

Paranormal Reverse Harem Romance

Completed Series

Warning: This series has one strong woman and four dangerously sexy immortal men. She's been their fated mate in every life they've lived and they refuse to live one without her. Read this series if you like why choose romance with a paranormal twist and hunky guys times four!

.

Masquerade Club Series

Dark Contemporary Romance

Completed Series

A contemporary saga with a side dish of spice and a second chance romance for two people you'll never forget. The Masquerade Club is exclusive and available only for the ultra-rich where all your dreams and fantasies come true. Join the party and fall in love with Connor and Katherine in this angst-ridden suspense-filled series.

.

ABOUT THE AUTHOR

Lilith Darville is a *USA Today* bestselling author of dangerously delicious romance, including sizzling paranormal reverse harem. With over forty years of storytelling experience, her stories are guaranteed to make readers flush and blush.

lilithdarville.com

9 781998 127269